Barry Cru Man, in 1 numerous other books which followed. His most famous and best-loved New Zealand character is Sam Cash, who features in *Hang on a Minute Mate*, Crump's second book. Between them, these two books have sold over 400,000 copies and continue to sell at an amazing rate some 30 years later.

Crump began his working life as a professional hunter, culling deer and pigs in some of the ruggedest country in New Zealand. After the runaway success of his first book, he pursued many diverse activities, including goldmining, radio talkback, white-baiting, television presenting, crocodile shooting and acting.

As to classifying his occupation, Crump always insisted that he was a Kiwi bushman.

He published 25 books and was awarded the MBE for services to literature in 1994.

Books by Barry Crump

A Good Keen Man (1960)
Hang on a Minute Mate (1961)
One of Us (1962)
There and Back (1963)
Gulf (1964) – now titled *Crocodile Country*
Scrapwaggon (1965)
The Odd Spot of Bother (1967)
No Reference Intended (1968)
Warm Beer and Other Stories (1969)
A Good Keen Girl (1970)
Bastards I Have Met (1970)
Fred (1972)
Shorty (1980)
Puha Road (1982)
The Adventures of Sam Cash (1985)
Wild Pork and Watercress (1986)
Barry Crump's Bedtime Yarns (1988)
Bullock Creek (1989)
The Life and Times of a Good Keen Man (1992)
Gold and Greenstone (1993)
Arty and the Fox (1994)
Forty Yarns and a Song (1995)
Mrs Windyflax and the Pungapeople (1995)
Crumpy's Campfire Companion (1996)
As the Saying Goes (1996)
A Tribute to Crumpy: Barry Crump 1935–1996 is an anthology of tributes, with extracts from Crump's books, letters and pictures from his private photo collection.

All titles currently (1997) in print.

SCRAPWAGGON

Dinny and Watcher, city dustmen who also indulge in a spot of rubbish-disposal unknown to their Council, lead profitable and peaceful lives — apart from a few hassles with Dinny's neighbours, who don't appreciate the mountain of 'treasures' he's accumulated in his garden. Then Dinny's daughter turns up to stay. He and Watcher try every trick to move her on, but she's inherited her Dad's obstinate streak, and soon she too is on the scrapwaggon.

Irate neighbours try to ban the whole squalid set-up. The City Council learn of the racket. They also discover that Dinny and Watcher aren't so easily sacked after all. . . .

Scrapwaggon, first published in 1965, is Barry Crump in top form. Dinny and Watcher are two of his most memorable creations. Old friends will find them just as hilarious on second meeting; new readers are promised a load of fun on every page.

Give a man a yard and he'll take the whole blasted street. . . .

Harry Taggit, in the back bar of Alf Cooper's pub.

BARRY CRUMP

SCRAPWAGGON

Illustrated by Roger Hart

Hodder Moa Beckett

First published in 1985 by Beckett Publishing

This edition published in 1997

ISBN 1-86958-542-9

© 1985 Barry Crump

Published by Hodder Moa Beckett Publishers Limited
[a member of the Hodder Headline Group]
4 Whetu Place, Mairangi Bay, Auckland, New Zealand

Typeset by TTS Jazz, Auckland

Cover photo: Fotopacific

Printed by Wright and Carman (NZ) Ltd, New Zealand

All rights reserved. No part of this publication may be reproduced or transmitted in any form or by any means, electronic or mechanical, including photocopying, recording, or any information storage and retrieval system, without permission in writing from the publisher.

Contents

TEN CHAPTERS
NUMBERED FROM ONE TO TEN

*with subtitles
which you'll see when you
come to them*

Among the events faithfully recorded in this book there is reference to a gentleman called Mr Bung Sumple, and in case there's going to be any fun poked at him about his name, I'd better tell you right now that he wasn't christened Bung Sumple by embittered parents or anything like that. His real name is Eugene Sumple. The Bung was tacked onto him because he couldn't sing quite as well as Bing Crosby when he was a young bloke. He gave up singing years ago but never managed to do the same with the nickname.

B.C.

Give a man a yard . . .

ONE
Give A Man A Yard . . .

Among the sedate respectability of the homes in Essentry Crescent on the borders of the city, there was a Number 17. And nobody who passed along Essentry Crescent failed to stop for a second astonished look at Dinny Virtue's place. It was a truly arresting sight. Some of the remarks inspired by the sight include:

"I suppose you'd get used to it in time."

"Hell!"

"What a beaut!"

"It's an offence against decency."

And, "I wonder if there's a distributor-shaft for my old Kelthorpe in there?"

Dinny Virtue was a Refuse Disposal Officer who was considerably stronger on collection than disposal. He'd never been able to distinguish between the perks and the junk, an inability that affects many of us.

At first the perks had been more or less catalogued in long rows from end to end of Dinny's half-acre yard, but "Furniture" had long since overlapped on one side into "Mechanical", and into the fence on the other. "Trunks and Boxes" had been dragged out and scattered. "Books and Toys" had been spilt out of "Trunks and Boxes" and the whole glorious tangle was festooned with the pages of wet books, kapok, and feathers. "Tents and Canvas" had been unrolled and blown into odd corners of the yard. It was no longer possible to tell where "Domestic" was originally centred, a very popular heap. The whole thing had become one great "General", and when Dinny had been unable to go any further along or out he went up, piling junk on junk. It would be safe to say that science, art, and workmanship have not yet achieved the outrageous effect that Dinny had created by accident. And it was difficult to ignore the crazy feeling that he'd once got hold of some inside information that one day there was going to be a terrible shortage of old bed-wires and soggy portraits of the Royal Family.

Dinny's relationships with his neighbours were generally pretty uncertain, but few of the people around hadn't at one time or another called on him for something they needed, though he'd known them to ransack stores and warehouses from one end of the city to the other before coming to him for some unprocurable bit or piece. The City Council engineers themselves had been known to blushingly call on Dinny and request permission to search for some unobtainable part or piece of machinery they'd thrown out years before. Looking across that magnificent conglomeration you just knew that what you wanted, whatever it was, was in there somewhere. No one had ever been able to prove it wasn't.

Although Dinny's interest in his collection of perks was largely amateur, the junk that had passed through his yard had practically paid for the middle-aged house that stood amongst it. A rumour, probably started by one of his singularly humourless neighbours, claims that the landlord he used to rent the place from had returned from a visit abroad to find himself faced with selling out cheap, or shifting Dinny out. Even if this were the truth, he probably got off pretty lightly, all things considered. An extension of the same rumour claims that the day Dinny paid his deposit on the house, property values in Essentry Crescent dropped by a clean fifteen per cent. But it's a free country.

Dinny Virtue ignored all these side-effects of his activities and went quietly about his own business, which was considerable.

Bung Sumple, a gentleman who'd survived twenty-eight faultless years in the City Corporation Valuer's office, was faced with the formidable task of evaluating the property at 17 Essentry Crescent, during a routine survey. There was promotion due to Mr Sumple in the near future, and despair on his brow as he read through yet another draft of the report he was trying to compose:

The property situated at 17 Essentry Crescent, N.E. 1, owned by Mr Dinford Reginald Virtue, is considered a local eyesore. No degree of accurate evaluation is possible, and although the building itself (built August, 1944) appears sound, as far as it is possible to ascertain, the property is unlikely to become a saleable proposition in the foreseeable future. . . .

Mr Sumple screwed up the report and threw it into his wastepaper basket, along with the earlier drafts. Then he swore, for the first time that year, at the wasted time he was going to have to catch up on, and went home to swear again at his wife.

Dinny woke up very carefully with the feeling that his eyelids were stitched together. He had a hangover. But he knew how to handle hangovers. He had a method of sneaking past while they weren't watching. He lay very still for a few moments getting the hang of it. This one was a beaut, about force-six on his private hangover-scale.

With the very top-front edge of his brain he thought about some plastic bags he'd brought home yesterday, and reached slowly out with one hand to feel along the side of the bed. His fingers closed round the neck of the bottle and he drew it slowly out of the boot it was jammed into. Then he sat up, swung his legs over the side of the bed, heaved one blurred eye half open and raised the bottle in a single smooth movement. Then somebody started knocking on the back door and ruined everything.

For a ghastly moment he was caught unawares. Before he

could get his mind shut the hangover surged up from behind him, speared through his brain, arc-welded his eyeballs and short-circuited his whole nervous system. An alarm sang in his ears and his stomach fell up and down inside him as though it was in a washing machine. He put the bottle on the floor with a thump that ran up his arm and caused the walls of his head to cave in, and rammed a handful of blanket into his face to stop it from exploding. His heart tripped and fell and his own fists began shaking themselves in his face. He thought very hard about the plastic bags and waited for it to pass. Dinny was in a bad way, and somebody was still knocking on the back door. If he hadn't wanted to see who it was he'd have probably hidden in his blanket and waited till they went away. But he hardly ever got visitors.

The hangover eventually sank away and perched restlessly in the back of his neck, as though daring him to make a false move. He got to his feet and glided carefully to the bedroom doorway, with his eyebrows held hard high on his forehead to hold back the headache. Down the hall and out through the kitchen. He throttled the door handle for a few moments to get control of the shakes and then drew the door open. There was a girl standing there.

She was about twenty-two or three, Dinny guessed. Beside her on the path was a fairly big suitcase he could have got her thirty bob for if she wanted to sell it. In her off-side hand she held a shopping bag kind of thing, with a green scarf spread over the top of whatever filled it and tucked in round the sides. The bag was Australian bullock-hide, worth about twelve bob with the scarf thrown in. Her jacket, blouse and skirt weren't new but there was still plenty of wear left in them. Twenty-five and six the lot, to the jumble-sale bloke on Thursday. Brownish kind of hair and fairly new shoes (not worth handling these days), and that was about it. She was about the same height as the handle of the swamp-hook leaning against the wall by the door and looked a bit nervous on it; picking at a big button on the front of her coat and staring at him as though the hangover was visible.

She didn't speak at once and Dinny wasn't in any hurry, so he left it to her. He rarely had a visitor like this, even if she had come to the wrong place, which nobody had ever done before. Maybe one of the Jehovah's Witnesses? — No, they always hunt in packs. Saleswoman? — Not a very good one if she was. He remembered the Welfare Officer who'd called in once to see if he had any kids living there. Could be, but a bit innocent-looking for that caper really. Quite a tidy little carcase on her, by the look of things.

No, he couldn't place this one at all. He was just about ready to give in and ask when she spoke.

"Hello Father," she said.

"Uh — What??"

"Don't you remember me? I'm Leila."

"Er — Oh yeah. Sure. How are you?"

"Aren't you pleased to see me?"

"Yeah, 'course I am. You just took me by surprise for a moment." He looked around and up the junk-lined path towards the gate. "Where's your mother?" he asked suspiciously.

"Mother died two months ago."

"Hell," said Dinny. " — I mean, that's real tough. 'Struth. You'd better come in and sit down for a while."

He had to let her carry her own bags. If he'd bent over to pick them up just then his head would have rolled off his shoulders, slopped onto the ground and seeped away. He led her into the kitchen and managed to pull a couple of chairs out from the table. They sat down.

"I didn't know about it," he said. "Haven't heard from any of you for — let's see — eleven, nearly twelve years. You were only a little bit of a . . ." Dinny's voice trailed off as the hangover thundered back again. She reached over to put her hand on his arm and he pulled it away so sharply the jolt set his eyeballs on fire.

"I understand how you feel, Father," she said gently.

When the pain in his head subsided until it merely felt like someone scrubbing the inside of his cranium with a wire brush, he said: "Where'd it happen?"

"It was cancer," said the girl. "She was in hospital for the last three months. They kept her under sedatives. She wasn't in any pain at the end."

"That's nice," said Dinny absently. "Where's — whatsisname?"

"He went off with a lady friend two days after mother was admitted to hospital," she said primly.

"Pretty good at that, isn't he?" observed Dinny.

"I had to stay on and attend to all the arrangements. I tried to get in touch with you because I knew you'd want to be there for the funeral, but I couldn't find a trace of you."

"Probably just as well," said Dinny. "I don't go for these emotional do's much. They upset me," he added quickly.

"It's taken me two weeks to find you," she said. "The police helped me in the finish, after I told them how urgent it was. It's marvellous how helpful people are when you're in trouble."

"Very decent of you to go to all that trouble to let me know," said Dinny.

"Oh it wasn't too bad really," she said. "I had a little money to tide me over."

"Well, drop in any time you feel like it," said Dinny generously. "I always like a bit of a yarn about old times." He just wanted to crawl away and lie down for a while and keeping up this polite conversation was becoming too much of a strain on his depleted reserves.

"But I've come to live with you, Father," said the girl.

"Like hell you have," said Dinny, taken by surprise again. "I mean, I can't have women living here."

"You're my father," she said, as though that solved everything. "There's nowhere else for me to go. I won't be in your way, and I can make myself quite useful." She glanced around the kitchen, an indoor replica of the yard outside.

"Look," said Dinny, "I'm sorry. You just can't stay here. It's absolutely out of the question."

"But you're my father," she repeated.

"I might be your father," argued Dinny weakly, "but I haven't seen you for twelve years. We're practically strangers. Your mother wouldn't want you staying here either."

"Mother told me to come," she said with an air of finality.

Dinny had had all he could stand. He got unsteadily to his feet and stumbled across the kitchen. "She would," he muttered.

"Do you mind if I do a bit of tidying up?" she asked meekly. "I don't want to barge in, but I'd enjoy having something to do."

"Go for your life," croaked Dinny, turning away to his bedroom.

"Is there a room I can put my things in?"

Dinny waved weakly up the hall towards the two spare rooms and closed his door behind him.

He sat on the edge of the bed. His head felt like an old knot someone had been trying to pick undone with a sack-needle.

His mind always seemed to dissolve when he needed it for something important, and now, just when he needed all his wits about him, he had the added handicap of one of his worst hangovers. He picked up the wine bottle, and then put it down again and went along to the bathroom for a wash. On his way back to the bedroom he saw Leila out in the kitchen tidying up around the sink.

"You know I'm only a garbage-collector?" he called out to her.

"I wondered where all the things came from," she said.

"What'll all your friends say when they find out your old man's a garbage-collector?"

"I haven't got any friends here," she replied. "And I don't have friends who care about things like that anyway."

Dinny went into the bedroom and drank from the wine bottle. Then he went back to the kitchen.

"I'm a very heavy drinker," he said. "I get drunk all the time."

"I can see you need someone here to look after you," she said. "It's too much for anyone, working and running a home too. Lots of people turn to drink when things get too much for them like this."

Dinny closed the bedroom door behind him and sat on the bed for a while. He was losing ground, and he didn't like the look of it.

When he came out again Leila was busy wiping down the table, scraping at the worst places with a knife. It was the first time Dinny had seen the whole surface of that table since he'd brought it home a year ago. It didn't look any better to him for being clean.

"I think it's only fair to tell you I've been in gaol," he announced. "I can't ask a young girl like you to live with a hardened criminal."

"Have you really?" she said interestedly. "We'll have to rehabilitate you."

"Drunk and disorderly," said Dinny hopefully.

"How long were you in gaol?"

"Four hours . . ."

"What's it like?"

Without answering Dinny returned to the bedroom to try and think of something else. He took two three-gulp drinks from the wine bottle, saw that it was nearly empty, and finished it off. Then he had to wait for his stomach to settle before he could go on with his thinking. When he went back to the kitchen for another go, she was busy throwing the plastic bags he'd brought home yesterday into a big cardboard box she'd got from somewhere.

"I'm getting married again!" he almost shouted.

No answer.

"To a widow. With eight kids!"

As soon as he'd said it he knew he'd overdone the kids. But she didn't seem to think so.

"Wonderful! I love children. Isn't it lucky? I'll be able to baby-sit for you."

"But we're going to live in Spain," he announced triumphantly. He waited to see what she was going to say about that one. She said:

"Help me carry this box outside, will you please, Father."

Obediently Dinny went to help his daughter carry the box outside. When he realised he was being practically ordered around in his own house he almost dropped his end of the box, but they were nearly out to one of the rubbish-heaps by then anyway. His favourite and most recent acquisitions usually enjoyed a brief term inside the house before finding their way outside, and here she was, within half an hour of barging in, turfing stuff out with complete disregard for its value. He threw the box angrily on to the heap. Leila retrieved it and began to shake it empty.

"I'll need this again," she said. "There's lots more rubbish to come out."

"Look," said Dinny desperately, "I might as well tell you the truth right now. I just can't afford to keep you here. I haven't got any money. I'm heavily in debt. I — I lost it all at the races. I'm a terrible gambler . . ."

"It's nice of you to take me into your confidence like this,

Father," she said sweetly. "As a matter of fact I might be able to help. I'm quite good at figures. Let's go through your books later, shall we?"

"Don't keep books," he said ungraciously.

"You must have a bank book," she said. "We can start with that. Tomorrow, when you've got over your shock."

"We're not starting with anything," snapped Dinny. "You can just . . ." But he couldn't think exactly what it was she could just, so he stalked back into the refuge of his bedroom. He knew he hadn't said enough, but at the same time he had the uncomfortable feeling that he'd said too much.

There was only one thing left to do. He'd have to go and see his partner, Watcher, about it. He kicked off his slippers and shoved his feet into his shoes as though he was trying to stamp them out. Then he strode out through the kitchen, determined not to say another disastrous word till he'd talked it over with Watcher. Leila was standing on a chair taking things off the mantelpiece and putting them down on the table.

"Going out?" she enquired.

"No," said Dinny cleverly.

"I'll cook those sausages in the cupboard for dinner, with potatoes and onions. When shall I expect you back?"

"I don't know."

He slammed the door behind him but it bounced open again.

He felt strangely foolish as he strode indignantly down his junk-lined path to the gateway, like a man who's come out with odd shoes on.

"Watcher'll have this fixed up in no time," he told himself hopefully.

Leila closed the kitchen door and smiled thoughtfully to herself. She liked her father, she decided. The prospect of living here was quite a pleasant one. Dinny would be all right once he got used to the idea.

Preamble

TWO

PREAMBLE

To say that Watcher Amble was unusual would be no more inaccurate than any other description of him. People seldom realised how little they knew about Watcher unless it was actually pointed out to them. He'd talk freely and sensibly on any subject you liked, except himself. And when there was anything to cover up he could cover it up so thoroughly that an eye-witness would be tempted to doubt the evidence of his own observations.

For example not more than a handful of people ever knew that his name hadn't always been Watcher Amble. The "Amble" was original, but the combination of his real christian name with it lent itself so irresistibly to a variety of ludicrous nicknames that he never even gave his proper name on official forms and things. And his signature was a tiny scribble that would have given a graphologist cross-eyed nightmares.

He'd left his never-mentioned home environs at the earliest legal age and raced his name from place to place, but it always seemed to catch up with him. Then he got a job in a factory where he had to sit all day watching for foul-ups on a fast-moving production line. His workmates, a pretty rough bunch, misunderstood but respected his reasons for not wanting to divulge his name. At first they referred to him as The Watcher, and then it became just Watcher. And for over twenty-five years he'd stuck to this, the first unembarrassing nickname he'd ever had.

It was hard to imagine that Watcher had ever worked anywhere but on the City Council refuse-collection gangs, or lived anywhere but in his hut made from two obsolete tramcars. He blended so perfectly with his surroundings that it was easy to imagine he'd been picked up with the first load of refuse ever collected and stayed in the game ever since.

This was the man Dinny was coming to consult about the problem of his daughter arriving to live with him. Dinny had worked with Watcher for several months before finding out that he was a pretty decent sort of a bloke, when he let you get to know him. For four years Dinny and Watcher had been partners, workmates, and friends.

"Come in," said Watcher. "How's things, Dinny?"

"Been better," said Dinny grimly.

"Seen you looking better. Still crook from last night eh?"

"Yeah."

"We did knock it around. I was a bit seedy myself this morning. Think I've got a bottle here somewhere."

Watcher opened a cupboard and got out a bottle of dry sherry. He put it on the table.

"Here, rip a bit of that into you."

"Where's your glasses?"

"No sense dirtying glasses for just the two of us," said Watcher.

"I'll wash 'em," said Dinny.

"That's what you always say, then you forget at the last minute and I've got to do them."

"I don't ask you to wash up at my place, do I?"

"Okay," said Watcher. And he got two dirty glasses off a shelf and slid them on to the table, the dirtiest one towards Dinny. Dinny absently reached over for the cleaner glass, wiped his thumb round the rim and poured himself a drink.

"We're in the cart," he announced.

"What's up?"

Dinny told him all about how his daughter had turned up from twelve years ago and was trying to move in and live with him. By the time he'd finished, the wine in the bottle was down to the bottom of the DRY SHERRY on the label. He waited for Watcher to say something.

"Didn't know you'd ever been married," he said. "And a daughter, too!"

"Yeah, I've been married," admitted Dinny. "Couldn't stand the wife any longer in the finish so she left me and ran off with a poultry farmer. The bottom fell out of eggs not long after that, and they went away down south somewhere. I got a letter from her once, asking if I'd take her and the kid back and forgive them. I dropped her a line saying okay but she wrote back that she wasn't really serious, just wanted to know if I would or not. That's the last I heard of them, till now." Dinny drank from his glass and waited for Watcher to solve everything.

"Well what do you reckon?" asked Dinny impatiently.

"Don't see that there's any problem," said Watcher, bunging the cork back into the bottle.

"No problem!" shouted Dinny, grabbing the bottle and pulling the cork out again.

"No," said Watcher. "As you said, she's cleaning up your house for you, and that's something it could use. I've noticed it getting a bit untidy over there the last week or two."

"She's clearing all my gear out of the house," corrected Dinny. "And a lot of that stuff's perishable. And what about our organisation we've built up over the years? What about our conference tonight on the Parnell contract? Do you think we're going to be able to hold business conferences with her listening in on our plans? I tell you she's going to disrupt our whole organisation!"

Watcher shared the last of the sherry out between the two glasses and put the empty bottle on the floor.

"See what you mean," he said. "It could get awkward."

"It's awkward already, I tell you. She thinks she's here to stay."

"Can't throw your own flesh and blood out on the street."

"I'd throw her out quick enough," growled Dinny, "but I don't think she'd go. She never bothers to come near me for twelve years, and then as soon as she's stuck for somewhere to live she comes runnin', expecting me to welcome her with open arms."

"Bit of a problem all right," admitted Watcher sagaciously.

"Well, what are we goin' to do about it?"

"Hard to say without seeing her," said Watcher. "What's she look like?"

"I hardly know her, I tell you. We're strangers. I haven't seen her since she was about six or seven years old."

"How old is she now?"

"'Bout nineteen or twenty."

"Good looker?"

"Nothin' startling."

"Look," said Watcher. "Tell you what, you go on home and I'll drop round later. Just on a chance visit like. After I've had a look at the situation we'll work out what's the best way to handle it."

"No fear," said Dinny. "I'm not goin' back there on me own. You can come with me."

"That's no good. We've got to be subtle about it. Don't want her to think she's got us rattled. You just go home and act as if nothing's happened. And don't say or do anything till we've had a conference about it later."

"Okay, but I don't like it. You haven't got another bottle of grog anywhere around, have you?"

"No more grog," said Watcher authoritatively. "We've got to keep a clear head for this. We'll need all our wits about us."

"Well, don't leave it too long before you come over," said Dinny.

"Be there in an hour," Watcher assured him.

And he was. He found Dinny sitting sullenly at the kitchen table while Leila hurried busily back and forth between the rubbish-heap and the room she'd chosen for herself with boxes of "rubbish". She was pleased to meet Watcher, made them a cup of tea, and left them alone. They sat in the unfamiliar kitchen and talked about the Job. After about half an hour Watcher had seen enough. He whispered to Dinny to come over to his hut after tea. Then he slunk out. Dinny sat on alone in the kitchen wondering what was going to happen. The girl came down the passage with another armful of his gear.

"Oh! Has your friend gone? I didn't say goodbye to him."

"He doesn't like women," said Dinny shortly.

"What a shame. He's such a nice man too," she sighed. "He must have had an unhappy love affair in his past." And she went out with her load, leaving Dinny sitting there with pursed lips and eyes.

He put in a couple of hours sorting through a new box of perks in the wash-house. He usually enjoyed looking over new perks, but this lot seemed to be nothing but junk. He went through the motions all the same, and pretended not to hear when Leila called out that his dinner was on the table. She didn't call out again and after a while he was so curious that he had to go through to the kitchen for a look.

His dinner was on the table. Leila's plate, knife and fork had been washed up and put away. He could hear her sweeping in her room up the passage. He wasn't going to eat any of her fancy grub. It could stay there till it went rotten for all he cared. He went over to the table to see what she'd cooked. Then he took a quick bite off the end of one of the sausages to see if it had been cooked properly. It had, but now there was a big bite mark, so he had to eat the rest of the sausage to destroy the evidence. He carefully arranged some mashed potato and onion over the place on the plate where the sausage had been, so as not to give her the impression he was going to let her cook for him.

It's funny about sausages. They're not like most other meat. Nobody remembers how many slices or hunks of beef or pork or mutton they've put on a plate, but it's different with sausages. If someone cooks six sausages and puts three on each of two plates, they remember. And if one's missing they're likely to notice. Dinny hadn't realised this about sausages before. He thought it over for a few moments and eventually decided to confuse her. He'd take a little from the potatoes and a little from the onions, to make her think she'd put out a smaller meal than she really had. He could lick the fork clean afterwards and leave everything just as it was. She'd never have a clue that he'd even touched her meal.

But it didn't work. For a start he accidentally took too much potato and tried to spread what was left over more of the plate. That made it look too flat so he left the potato for the time being and ate a few more onions to get the proportion right. Then he scraped the potato back into a sort of heap but there was potato left all over the plate where it had been. He carefully licked the plate clean all round the outside and started again to rearrange everything.

He was so engrossed that he failed to hear her coming along the hall. When she walked into the kitchen Dinny was sitting with his chin on the table, trying to build a hollow pile of cold mashed potato on his plate with the handle of his fork.

"Has your dinner got cold?" she enquired concernedly. "What a shame! The very first meal I've cooked for you, too. I was sure you must have heard me call you. If I'd known you were so busy I could have kept it warm for you."

Dinny slowly raised his head from the table but not his eyes.

"Would you like me to heat it up again for you?" she asked. "It wouldn't take a moment."

"Not hungry," he mumbled, getting up from the table.

"The way you were rattling your plate I thought I'd have to cook you some more," she laughed, turning back up the passage. "Just leave your plate on the bench, I'll fix it later."

Dinny grabbed his coat from behind the door, snatched up the two remaining sausages and ate them on the way round to Watcher's hut. He wouldn't have to put up with it much longer, once Watcher got to work.

Watcher had his lamp lit and a bottle ready. In fact the bottle was almost a third over-ready by the time Dinny arrived. Watcher poured him a drink.

"Got any ideas?" demanded Dinny.

"Plenty," said Watcher. "But she's going to be a tough nut to crack, all the same. Might take a bit of time."

"Why don't we just go round and tell her to get the hell out of it?" said Dinny impatiently. "That wouldn't take much time."

"Make you look a proper joe, wouldn't it," observed Watcher. "No, that's not the answer. You can't just kick her out. It's out of the question."

"Can't I!" said Dinny hotly. "If she's still here this time tomorrow I'll . . ."

"Cut it out," interrupted Watcher. "If you were going to be able to throw her out you'd have done it by now."

"It's a free country," insisted Dinny. "I'll have her out of there if I have to get the cops on to her. They'll shift her!"

"She's not twenty-one yet and you're still responsible for her. And the cops'll never interfere in a family row unless someone's getting knocked around. Let's face it, you're not going to be able to throw her out and you know it."

"Why not?" Dinny wanted to know.

"Because you're her father and she's not doing anyone any harm."

"She's only disrupted me whole life, that's all. A man's got a right to his privacy."

"And she's got a right to have somewhere to live," said Watcher.

"She's perfectly capable of getting a job and somewhere of her own to live. I don't care what you say."

"When she gets over losing her mother she'll probably do that."

"It didn't take *me* this long to get over losing her mother," said Dinny ungraciously. "So you reckon there's nothing we can do about it," he challenged, draining his glass. "You're just going to sit back and let her overrun me whole life. Wreck all our plans for making big money. Tie our hands. Rob us of our freedom, and the little bit of fun we get out of life. Take over everything we've built up over the years. A fine mate you turned out to be."

"Now take it easy," said Watcher, pouring a splash into Dinny's glass and a lot into his own. "You're getting carried away again. You'll never break into big business if you're going to throw a Charlie every time a bit of a problem crops up. You have to sit quietly back with a bottle of plonk and nut out all the angles. That's the way fortunes are made."

"But you just said there was nothing we could do about it."

"I didn't say any such thing. I simply pointed out that you can't turf her out, that's all. We've got to be subtle about it. — Now listen. I reckon the best thing that could happen would be for her to leave off her own bat. What we've got to do is make her *want* to go. That way everybody'll be happy. But as long as she doesn't want to go she won't think about doing it."

Dinny thought it over while he topped up his glass.

"I reckon you might just have stumbled on to something there," he said thoughtfully. "All we've got to do is belt her around a bit — starve her out . . ."

"No, no, no! You'd never belt anyone around and you'd starve yourself to death before you'd see a mad dog go without a feed, you know that. That's why you'll never make a fortune without me to keep you from going off half-cocked."

"Well what, then?"

"We'll have to make it so she can't stand the place," said Watcher. "Everyone's got things they don't like. What we've got to do is find out what this daughter of yours doesn't like most, and give her the works."

"Don't think she's too keen on the booze," said Dinny helpfully.

"The trouble with things like booze and gambling is that they're liable to back-fire on you," said Watcher thoughtfully.

"How do you work that out?"

"She might take it the wrong way, and think she has to save us from our weaknesses. We don't want to risk making a soul-saver out of her. Once they get the idea they're really needed Old Nick himself wouldn't shift them. I've seen it happen before. The booze might work but we'd better try one or two other things first."

"What things?"

"First of all we'd better find out as much about her as we can. What happened after I left your place this afternoon?"

"She just went on throwing out all my valuable equipment," said Dinny.

"What did she say after I left?" insisted Watcher. "She must have said something."

"Well she said what a nice bloke you were."

"Hmmm, that makes it tough."

"What do you mean, makes it tough?"

"Never mind. What else did she say?"

"She said you must have had a messed-up love-life,"

remembered Dinny. "You see! She's started on sex already. Before we know what's happening she'll have young blokes hanging around, poking about with all my valuable gear, climbing in and out the windows all hours of the night. And then she'll get herself into trouble and I'll get the blame for not keeping an eye on her."

"Hey, now," laughed Watcher. "You've got your tail in the air again. Keep calm, this is serious business. What made her say that?"

"Say what?"

"About me having a mixed-up love-life."

"I don't know. I think it might have been something I said about you not having much to do with women."

"You're getting pretty chummy on it, aren't you? How come you got to talking about men and women with her in the first place?"

"We weren't," said Dinny. "That's all that was said. I hardly spoke to her all afternoon."

"Anything else happen?"

"No. I spent a fair while going through that new box of gear we picked up on Friday. She just cooked a feed and went on throwing things outside."

"What's her cooking like? They often use that to get a man won over."

"All right I suppose," said Dinny uncomfortably. "Didn't take much notice of it."

"Have to watch out for things like that. You didn't eat any of her cooking did you?"

"What? — No, no," lied Dinny, and he drained his glass.

"Good. We'll have to be careful not to get too friendly with her, especially you. We don't want sentiment entering into it. Try not to let her get into the habit of doing anything she might think makes her indispensable."

"I'm not likely to go getting friendly with her," growled Dinny. "I wouldn't . . ."

"Okay, okay. Keep an eye on her. Watch for anything that might give us an idea what puts her teeth on edge. There's bound to be something. I'll think about it tonight and we'll have another conference at work tomorrow. We've got that bloody Horne Bay run. I'll pick up the scrapwaggon and come over to your place about half past nine."

"Do you think I ought to tell her you're going to move in and we need the spare room? Or something?"

"No. We don't want her to get so much as a whisper that we're up to something. If she gets suspicious the whole thing's had it."

When Dinny got home Leila was hanging up some washed clothes in the kitchen. She put on a cup of tea.

"I didn't know whether to wait up for you or not," she said.

"You don't have to worry about me," he growled.

"Of course I worry about you. I know how you feel just now. It's a terrible strain. What you need is a jolly good sleep."

As he stalked off to his bedroom she called after him: "Your cup of tea's ready, would you like me to bring it in to you?"

"No, I wouldn't," he snarled, jamming his bedroom door shut.

He got into bed feeling as though he'd spent all day going round tying tins on to dogs' tails.

Scrapwaggon

THREE
Scrapwaggon

Watcher picked up the scrapwaggon from the Council depot and arrived to collect Dinny just after nine o'clock. Dinny wasn't ready. Watcher blew the horn and sat in the truck to wait.

It didn't really matter what time they started in the mornings as long as they got their work done. They had their runs worked out so neatly that they seldom did more than four hours' work on any day. They'd worked out all the available short-cuts and organised quite a few that weren't available. Then they'd had to arrange some interesting methods of passing the time they'd saved to make it look as though they were working hard.

"It doesn't matter how little you actually do," Watcher often said. "As long as it looks like a lot everyone's happy."

But they had to be careful not to let their boss run away with the idea that they could handle any extra work. It was a knack of being flat-out both ways at once.

Dinny emerged from his jungle of perks looking worried and climbed into the truck.

"Slept in, eh," grinned Watcher. "Have to dock your pay for that."

Dinny didn't answer so he let it drop.

They did a street, one driving and the other collecting the tins of trash in turns. Then they pulled into one of their private sub-depots to go through some interesting stuff a doctor had thrown out. It wasn't as good as it had first looked. Mostly old books and magazines and medicine-bottles.

"Deceptive, this stuff," said Dinny. "It doesn't look much but some of these books might sell for three or four bob."

"Better leave it," said Watcher. "We lose too much on the handling with that kind of stuff."

They got into the truck for a conference and a snort from the "survival kit" they kept behind the seat (a thermos of sweet sherry, for use only in emergencies such as hangovers, wet days, time to pass, opportunities, and conferences).

"How's it going at home?" asked Watcher, passing Dinny the thermos for the first drink.

"No good," said Dinny. "She thinks she's there for keeps all right. I didn't know where I was when I came out of my room this morning."

"Got the place cleaned up, eh?"

"No, cluttered up. She's got her washing hangin' all over the kitchen. Have to keep duckin' under things every time I want to move round."

"Change from stepping over things," observed Watcher, taking the thermos and drinking from it. "We'll have to keep a lookout for a thermos that's not broken. The rust and stuff in this one's turning the plonk sour."

"But they're underclothes and things," insisted Dinny. "It's not right."

"She's your daughter," pointed out Watcher.

"That's what she said when I tackled her about it," said Dinny. "But it doesn't make it any better as far as I'm concerned. We'll have to get her out of it. I couldn't live with anyone like her, even if I wanted to. She's got the place looking like a morgue. There's no atmosphere in it any more."

"Plenty of atmosphere in a morgue," grinned Watcher. "Had a look round in one once."

"Never mind that, what are we going to do about Leila?"

"What was she like when you left this morning?"

"She woke me up with cups of tea three times. Just came

barging into me private room as though she owned the place."

"Sounds like a good worker."

"Too bloody good. That's the trouble," complained Dinny. "A man can't go on being bitchy at someone who never does anything wrong. She tries so hard to please me all the time it's gettin' on me nerves. And she thinks I'm just upset about her mother kickin' off."

"You haven't softened up on her, have you?" asked Watcher suspiciously.

"No I haven't, but it's against human nature to keep on ignoring someone all the time. I tell you we'll have to do something quick, before I pack up altogether."

"Think I've got an idea," said Watcher.

"What is it? I'll try anything."

"All this washing and cleaning up she's doing."

"What about it?"

"We're going to make her ashamed of us," announced Watcher.

"Huh?"

"We'll go round to your place for lunch. The sight of us in our working clobber and the old scrapwaggon here parked outside might just be enough to convince her we're not worth puttin' up with."

"I'll have a go at anything," said Dinny.

"Right. It's near enough to lunch time now. We'll stop on the way and pick up a bit more rubbish to top off the load. Got to make it look right. Keep your eye open for a couple of good ones, there's usually one or two along College Street."

Watcher screwed the top on the thermos and put it behind the seat. Dinny, who was behind the wheel, drove, while Watcher emptied a few extra cans of rubbish artistically along the top of the load.

"That'll do us," he said climbing into the cab beside Dinny.

"Looked like a few perks in the one before last. We'll go through it after lunch."

They pulled up at Dinny's place and got out of the truck. Watcher looked around the yard.

"Say, you're getting quite a collection here," he said admiringly. "Haven't seen some of this before. Where did it come from?"

"Inside," said Dinny shortly, going on up the path.

Watcher whistled softly, shook his head and followed Dinny. Leila came down the passage into the kitchen just as the two men were getting seated at the table. There was no washing hanging in the kitchen but there was a piece of rope strung twice across the room that Watcher hadn't seen before.

"Oh hello," she said pleasantly. "If I'd known you were coming home for lunch I could have got something ready for you. Have you got time for me to cook up something now?"

"We never eat lunch," grunted Dinny.

"Well I'll make you a cup of tea. You'll need something to keep you going."

"Thanks," said Watcher. "I could go a drink. Hope it's not too much trouble."

Dinny turned to stare at him. He was just going to say something when Watcher went on: "Dry work on the old rubbish cart, eh Dinny?"

"Er — yeah," stammered Dinny.

Leila poured their tea, put the milk and sugar on the table for them and then went to the back door. "Just call out if there's anything else you want," she said. "I'll be out by the fence. I'm clearing a place to put a clothesline."

"What the hell are you being nice to her for?" hissed Dinny as soon as she was gone. "You'll have her thinking . . ."

"Don't panic," said Watcher calmly. "I think you might have

been overdoing it a bit. If you talk to her like that all the time she'll end up thinking you're just a big gruff daddy whose bark's worse than his bite, and she won't take anything you say seriously."

Dinny was confused. "That's all very well for you, but you don't have to — shhh, here she comes."

Leila came in the door and caught them in the act of looking guilty.

"Is that your truck out on the road?" she asked.

"Yeah, that's the old scrapwaggon," said Watcher.

"We always park it out there," added Dinny.

"Could I go and have a look?" she asked. "I won't touch anything."

Dinny glanced at Watcher to see what he'd say to that.

"Sure, help yourself," said Watcher.

The girl went out and the two men sat in silence for a few moments. Then Watcher said: "Good legs eh?"

"Uh, what?"

"She's got a decent set of pins on her," said Watcher.

"I wish she'd use 'em to cart herself off somewhere," growled Dinny. "You can see what she's doing to the place, can't you?"

"Yeah. Wonder what she wanted to have a look at the scrapwaggon for?"

"Probably pretending to be interested in our work," said Dinny. "Let's get back and finish the run. At least we can talk out on the job without anyone listening in."

"Ar, you worry too much," said Watcher, following him outside.

"Where'd Leila go?" asked Watcher as they approached the truck.

"Probably took one look and went for her life," said Dinny. "Not much to look at at the best of times," said Watcher. "Well I'll

43

go to . . . Have a look at that!"

Leila was standing on the centre of the rear wheel of the scrapwaggon reaching into the back. She saw the men coming and held up a heavy old book for them to see.

"Look," she said. "A *Webster's Dictionary* in perfect condition. It must be worth quite a bit."

"What the hell are you doing up there?" shouted Dinny.

She dropped the book back into the rubbish and jumped down on to the footpath. "You said I could have a look, Father," she said scoldingly.

"We didn't mean you could climb all over the bloody thing," blurted Dinny.

Watcher had reached into the back of the truck for the book Leila had dropped. He passed it to her. "Here y'are," he said cheerfully. "It's all yours. Compliments of the management."

She took the book and ran to the house with it. Dinny looked suspiciously at Watcher. "What are you up to?" he demanded.

"We did tell her to help herself," said Watcher.

"You told her, you mean."

"Hmmm. Anyway that's one trick we can cross off our little list," said Watcher. He climbed into the truck.

"You mean her not being put off by the scrapwaggon?"

"Not only that," replied Watcher, "but that girl's a born scavenger if ever I saw one. A real chip off the old block."

"I don't believe it," said Dinny. "She's just pretending, to try and win us over so we'll let her stay. Anyway we've got her a bit rattled."

"Rattled?"

"The way she got upset when I told her to get off the truck," said Dinny smugly.

"She might be pretending about a lot of things," disagreed Watcher. "Everybody does, if it comes to that. But I don't think she was pretending about being interested in this load of stuff, and I don't think she was rattled either. No one could pretend that well about a thing that puts them off."

"What about all my good gear she threw out of the house?" asked Dinny.

"Did she throw out any really good stuff?"

"I haven't had a chance to check up on it yet, but . . ."

"Might pay you to look it over," said Watcher. "You are inclined to be a bit over-enthusiastic about perk-collecting, you know."

"Are you trying to tell me she's a better judge of perks than I am?" demanded Dinny hotly.

"No fear," said Watcher patiently. "No amount of talent could ever make up for your experience. You've got nothing to worry about there."

"Well what are we going to do now?"

"I think we'll try something else tonight," said Watcher.

"What?"

"Tell you about it in the pub after we take the truck in," said Watcher. "It'll take careful planning."

They dumped their load and collected, sorted and dumped the rest of the run. Then they took some new perks round to Dinny's place and threw them over the fence. Leila came out to see what they were doing but they told her they were in a hurry and drove off, leaving her peering into the pile of stuff they'd brought.

When she'd finished looking at the new perks Leila turned to go inside and caught a glimpse of somebody's face beside the curtain in a window of the house opposite. She waved and smiled. The curtain fell across the face. It must be the Mr Tweek she'd heard her father and Watcher talking about. Arthur Tweek had enjoyed a full and rewarding career as a traffic officer. His punctual efficiency; his devotion to duty and detail; his level-headed courage in the face of danger or emergency; his scrupulous fairness and courtesy in dealing with the public; the precision of his reports and the honest accuracy of his evidence, had been a source of irritation to everyone he worked on, everyone he worked for, and everyone he worked with, for almost forty years. He retired from the service at sixty with all the above-mentioned qualities in perfect running order.

Officer Tweek had been planning for his retirement at an age when most people are still wondering whether or not to get married. Perhaps it was just as well. A Mrs Tweek who'd survived this long would have been a woeful creature indeed.

Being a bachelor, efficient, willing, and intolerable, Officer Tweek was kept almost permanently on relieving duty. He would relieve officers away on holiday, or ill, or until they could be replaced. He was sent to places and functions where the local traffic men were overloaded with work. Anything to keep him on the move, and wherever he moved he irritated people. But this arrangement suited Officer Tweek nicely. The department not only supplied him with free lodgings wherever he went, but subsidised his search for a place to retire to.

Long before he retired he'd decided on the centre and the suburb that would suit him best. And he knew the distances he wanted to be from the shops, the bus-routes, the hospital, the sea, the courthouse, and other people. He chose the house and had two different valuers go over it twice — and had the courts go over the speculator he bought it from.

Officer Tweek (ret.) settled into his own home to enjoy the years of untroubled leisure he'd so conscientiously provided for. His privacy was shielded from the curiosity of his neighbours on either side by two boundaries of elegant thirty-foot black poplars, which wouldn't have to be trimmed for at least twenty years. And from his deck-chair on the front veranda he could choose between a view of his garden and the houses across the street, or the houses across the street and the top of the hills on the far side of the harbour. Mr Tweek had every reason to feel pleased with the foresight that had promised to make his retirement as unblemished as his working life had been. He settled down to wait for the end of his life with a clear conscience.

But Mr Tweek had not foreseen or provided for that particular brand of injustice that strikes a man down in his moment of triumph. He had scarcely had time to get his new neighbours properly antagonised when Dinny Virtue moved into Number 17, straight across the street from him.

Mr Tweek watched with apprehension, indignation, shock, and finally outrage, as Dinny added daily to the construction of the monstrous eyesore that dominated his only view.

Officer Tweek had risen up against this threat to the dignity of his retirement. He fought it with all the old fire that for almost forty years had rendered the nation's highways unpleasant for the innocent and guilty alike. He complained in triplicate to the proper authorities, and then went over their heads and complained in person. He consulted his solicitor. He presented petitions signed by nearly half the residents of Essentry Crescent. He studied the by-laws and the regulations. He enquired abroad for the owner of Number 17. He enlisted the support of his neighbours and quoted endlessly from the Regulations. He sent telegrams to his local M.P., letters to the editor, and urgent messages to *Truth*, demanding that something be done. He shouted at Dinny from the street. He complained about noise, nuisance, devaluation of properties, health, rats, hazards, victimisation, and the inefficiency of whoever he was complaining to.

He tried to sell his house.

There was nothing anyone could do about it. Dinny kept

himself to his yard, his job, himself, and later on his friend Watcher. He'd decided that the old codger across the road was nuts, and left it at that.

After more than eight years of campaigning the results of Mr Tweek's efforts added up to Dinny holding the honour of being the biggest nuisance in Essentry Crescent, after Mr Tweek. But he never gave up trying to find some way to have that man and his hideous rubbish swept off the face of his retirement. He couldn't even sell his house and go away from it all. After a life spent in the service of justice, Mr Tweek could get none for himself.

And now that man was openly living with a girl young enough to be his daughter.

After they'd put their truck in at the depot Dinny and Watcher adjourned to the pub.

"Well what's this new scheme of yours?" asked Dinny impatiently.

"Swearing," said Watcher. "I've been working it out. If we don't do it now it'll never work, she'd know we were just bunging it on."

"Swearing?" frowned Dinny. "You mean bad language?"

"Yeah. It's one thing not many women can take much of. We'll go round to your place after the pub. Pretend to be a bit shikker, not much, just enough to be merry."

"And start swearing?"

"Yeah."

"Why don't we take some grog and make a proper job of it?" suggested Dinny.

"No fear. We don't want to louse it up with a crook performance. We want to make her think we swear *all* the time, not just when we're drunk. We'll just bowl in and let rip with a few jokes and the odd word or two here and there, natural like.

Have to be careful not to overdo it."

"Okay," said Dinny dubiously. "I sure hope this works. Me nerves are packin' up on me."

"If it doesn't work we'll have to try something else," said Watcher. "The important thing is to work it so that when she does leave she won't be able to blame us."

They not quite rolled up at Dinny's place just on dark that evening. Leila was at the stove with steaming pots.

"Hello," she said. "I'm glad Mr Amble came. I've cooked enough for all of us. We can all eat together — unless you have some business to talk about."

There was a brief silence while Dinny and Watcher gathered their wits and their words. Then Dinny blurted: "D'you feel like any blasted tucker, Watcher?"

"Blowed if I know," replied Watcher.

"What the broodin' hell's this?" Dinny asked, looking at something under the table.

"Stew," said Leila calmly. "I was wondering about food. Would you like me to make out a list of the things we need?"

"Is there any broodin' grog in the broodin' place?" asked Dinny.

"Yeah, I'm as dry as a beggar," added Watcher politely.

"I haven't seen any round," said Leila. "Have you got any in your room, Father?"

"Broodin' hell," whispered Dinny. "No broodin' booze."

"Yeah. No brooding booze," echoed Watcher helpfully.

"Yeah," said Dinny. "We should bug — go back to the pub and get some."

Leila put some plates on the table. "If you're going to bugger off back to the pub for some grog you'll have to hurry. They've been closed for an hour," she said casually. "Will you have your bloody tucker now, or shall I keep it till you get back?"

She served them their food and they ate in a squirming silence. Watcher bolted his food and stood up.

"Well, it's getting late," he said. "Think I'll be getting back to me hut. Big day tomorrow. — Thanks for the feed, miss."

"You're welcome," she said pleasantly. "I hope Father brings you often."

"Yeah, well thanks a lot. See you in the morning, Dinny."

"Wait on," said Dinny desperately. "I think I'll just walk some of the way with you. I always like to get a bit of fresh air before I turn in."

They walked for a while in silence. Then Dinny said: "She was pretending that time all right."

"So were we — only she made a better job of it. Upstaged us good and proper."

"Wonder where she picked up all that language?" said Dinny. "I didn't think she'd know about things like that."

"She's not exactly a baby," Watcher reminded him. "And don't make any mistake about the kids these days. She could probably teach us a thing or two."

"You don't think she's one of them juvenile delinquents, do you?" asked Dinny in alarm.

"Not a show. She's just an ordinary girl who's been around a bit more than most, that's all. I'll tell you something else too, she's about the smartest piece of work I've come across in a long time."

"Well it looks like she's got us whacked, anyway," said Dinny despondently.

"Oh we're not whacked yet, by a long shot. She's just got us temporarily stonkered, that's all. We'll come up with something that'll rock her, don't worry."

"None of these ideas of yours seem to be working out," accused Dinny.

"Not on their own," admitted Watcher, "but all added up

together they'll have the same effect in the long run. We'll have to work on a completely different angle."

"What about the booze?" suggested Dinny. "We haven't tried that yet."

"Might be worth a try. There's no telling what might work. But she's probably livened that we're up to something by now. We'll have to be extra crafty about it."

"It's hard to imagine anyone who looks like that, being like that," said Dinny, kicking in wonder at a stone on the roadside.

"She's no different from anyone else," said Watcher. "One thing, we know she's quite capable of keeping her end up, whatever happens to her. She won't have a nervous breakdown on us, or anything like that."

"Yeah, but think what'd happen if she got some kind of foothold in our set-up."

Watcher laughed. "She has already, and a pretty strong foothold at that. But we'll come up with something, don't let it get you down. I'll just cut through here to my hut. See you in the morning, same time. I'll pick up the waggon. There's only the two-hour run tomorrow."

Two days later Bung Sumple's boss asked Bung for his still unwritten report. Mr Sumple promised to have it on his desk the following day without fail. The following day Mr Sumple spent his lunch hour and a half in the private bar of Alf Cooper's pub, and returned to the office in a condition which the typist described as "tiddly". He scribbled distractedly all over two report forms and his blotter, and then had to go home early with a violent headache.

One for a jack

FOUR
One for a Jack

It was over a week before they got the booze campaign organised. They'd been neglecting their side-lines and devoting too much of their time to trying to get rid of Dinny's daughter. Several small "contracts" for filling had to be attended to, and the new tyres on one of the Council trucks had to be changed for worn ones they'd collected from a trucking firm's garbage-heap. Forty sheets of old roofing-iron had to be dropped off a few at a time where a bloke they knew was building a boatshed.

"We'll try the booze on her as soon as we've got time to do it properly," said Watcher, passing a full dustbin up to Dinny on the truck.

"But in the meantime we're getting out of drinking form," complained Dinny. "Our boozing's fallen right off. And our organisation's being neglected. They've paid a contractor to do that Everton Street job I just about had lined up. That's five quid we could have picked up if we'd had time to arrange it properly. We hardly ever see each other these days."

"It's no use turning on the grog unless it's the real thing," said Watcher. "And if we wait a while before we try it she won't be so suspicious."

"It's all right for you," said Dinny. "You don't have to live with her."

"Ar, she's not all that bad," said Watcher.

"She had me playing bloody cards last night," said Dinny indignantly.

"Poker?"

"No. Strip-Jack-Naked," snarled Dinny. "A bloody kid's game."

"Not a bad game that," consoled Watcher. "Used to play it meself."

"Well I've got more to do with me time than play games. I've got a business organisation to look after. She's costing me a small fortune."

"You've got to admit she's made a fair bit of difference since she's been with us," said Watcher reasonably.

"Difference! You're telling me she's made a difference! I should have got the police on to her in the first place."

"It was no use then so it's too late to think about it now."

"Well I just hope this grog trick works, that's all. If it doesn't I'm going to sell out, lock, stock, and barrel, and take off somewhere."

"What? Give up all we've worked and strived to build up? One of the biggest perk-organisations in the country, and you want to walk off and leave it just like that?" Watcher was getting excited now.

"It's no use if I can't call me home me own," said Dinny. "A man's freedom comes first. It's no good amassing a fortune if you're not going to be free to enjoy it."

"You're a beaut," said Watcher. "You're enthusiastically unenthusiastic one minute, and the next you're enthusiastically enthusiastic again. You're too enthusiastic."

Dinny stood there on the trash-waggon, frowning over whether Watcher had just praised or abused him. Watcher leaned on the side of the truck and passed him up a cigarette to help him think.

"We haven't even tried the booze one yet, and you're already talking as though it was a complete flop. We haven't tapped our resources yet."

"Well when are we going to do it?" asked Dinny.

"Have to get the grog first. We'll need a fair bit, and our finances aren't too healthy at the moment. I had to pay back that six quid the bloke's wife paid us for those loads of filling. He reckoned there was too much paper in it and it blew all over the place."

"Why didn't you tell him to take a running jump at himself?"

"Couldn't argue with him. Threatened to complain to the Council about it."

"Hell. Best to pay up when they come at that," said Dinny. "We can't risk any complaints or they'll start keeping an eye on everything we do. I've got twenty quid at home anyway; we can use some of that for our grog."

"Twenty quid! Where'd you get it?"

"Well you know how people sometimes think my place is a junk yard?"

"Er — yeah."

"Well, people have been coming round looking for odd things while we've been out, and Leila's sold quite a bit of my best gear. I tore a strip off her when I found out, but she didn't seem to realise how serious it was."

"Hell man," said Watcher. "You should have told her to go ahead and sell as much as she likes. That's good business."

"I did," said Dinny, shuffling his feet in the rubbish on the back of the truck.

The big booze-up was organised in the greatest secrecy.

"If our security on this breaks down," said Watcher solemnly, "the blokes in the pub'll come round like flies for the party, and we don't want Leila to think it's an event. It's supposed to be our normal way of living."

They bought the grog over several days so as not to create any excitement in local drinking circles.

"You blokes are really hitting it along lately," said Alf Cooper the publican to Dinny, who'd called in for his second suitcase of bottles in the same afternoon. "I don't know how you stand up to it."

"We're used to it," said Dinny awkwardly. "We — er — it's a matter of practice."

They stored the grog in Watcher's hut under lock and key, and on the day set aside for its use they loaded it all into the scrapwaggon and covered it with sacks and trash. Then they drove to Dinny's place and parked the waggon outside the gate. It would be quite safe there till it was time to spring their surprise and get the truck back to the depot.

They had an hour or two to kill, so they prowled around in the yard, pretending to be looking for something. Leila made them cups of tea, which they insisted on having out in the fresh air and sunshine. And they were so careful not to make any slips about what was uppermost in both their minds that they hardly spoke to each other at all. Then as the time was drawing near, Leila came out to where they were squatting intently around a cracked motor-block and said: "The stuff you've got in the truck isn't stolen, is it?"

"No," said Dinny indignantly. "We paid hard cash for every drop of it."

"Don't know what you're talking about," said Watcher quickly.

"If it's drink and it's not stolen," she suggested, "why don't you bring it inside? It'll be getting terribly warm out there in the sun."

She helped them to carry it all in. Dinny lined up all the bottles on the bench and the mantelpiece in the kitchen, while Watcher took the scrapwaggon to the depot. He returned in a taxi so as not to miss anything. Dinny and Watcher sat at the table and opened a bottle of beer each.

"What's the party in aid of?" enquired Leila.

"We're returning to our old habits," Dinny said. Far too loudly.

"Oh? What habits are those?"

"We used to have a few drinks here every weekend," said Watcher.

"Drunken hoolies," corrected Dinny.

"Lasting for days," added Watcher.

"Weeks!" gloated Dinny. "*Orgies*!" he almost shouted.

"I wish you'd told me," said Leila. "I could have got some nice food to go with your drinks."

"We never eat when we're drinking," said Dinny.

"Don't touch food for days on end," said Watcher.

"Heavens. I hope you don't make yourselves ill," said Leila. "Perhaps I'd better go down to the store for some aspirins and something to settle stomachs, just in case."

"Never use any of that kind of stuff," said Dinny.

"Never need it," said Watcher.

"Don't want it," said Dinny.

"I don't suppose you'll want me hanging around then," she said. "I'll go off to the pictures if you like. Is there anything you want before I go?"

The men were silent.

"It's all right if I go out, isn't it?" she asked.

"Have to think about that," said Dinny, glancing at Watcher. "I think we'd better have a conference," suggested Watcher. They took their bottles of beer into Dinny's bedroom to hold a conference on what to do about Leila going off to the pictures.

"It's no good staging all this for her if she's not going to be here to see it," said Dinny.

"She's a bit young to be wandering around on her own late at night anyway, isn't she?" said Watcher concernedly. "Anything could happen to her."

"Friday night, too," said Dinny. "If anything happened to her we'd be responsible for letting her go out alone."

"You're her father, you know, Dinny. It's your responsibility."

"Yeah, that's right. But I can't *make* her stay home if she doesn't want to."

"We could carry on without her and be ready for when she gets back," said Watcher.

"I don't know, Watcher," said Dinny, drinking solemnly from his bottle. "I don't think I'd be able to relax and enjoy myself, seeing as how I'm responsible and all that. I'd be too worried. Sitting here boozin' while me only daughter's out goodness knows where on her own. It wouldn't be right."

Watcher drank from his bottle. "In that case there's only one course open to us," he said.

"What's that?"

"We'll have to give her the choice. We can't force her to stay, but if she wants to hang around and find out the truth about us, let it be her decision."

"You're dead right," said Dinny. "Let's go and tell her. *You* tell her," he added. "It's your idea, and I'm a bit hazy on the details. I might muck it up."

They went back to the kitchen, took their places at the table, filled their glasses and drank deeply. Leila was putting something on the stove.

"How was your conference?" she asked. "It looks serious."

Watcher cleared his throat. "We've been discussing this matter, your father and I, and we've decided that seeing as we're more or less your — er — guardians, we feel a bit responsible."

She just stood there looking puzzled. Watcher continued: "How old are you, lass?"

"What's that got to do with it?" she asked.

"We're not sure that a young girl like you ought to be going out on her own," said Dinny. "It mightn't be safe."

"Good heavens," she said. "I've been going out on my own ever since I was twelve years old. I'm eighteen, if you must know.

As a matter of fact I'll be nineteen next Wednesday week."

"We thought you might like to wait till one of us can come with you," lied Watcher.

"Oh that'd be nice," she said. "When?"

"Some time next week, when we've finished our booze-up," said Dinny. "Pour yourself a beer, seein' as it's your birthday next Wednesday week."

"Just one glass, though," added Watcher solicitously.

Leila got herself a glass from the cupboard and poured herself a drink from Dinny's bottle.

"It's awfully warm and frothy," she said, wiping her lips.

Dinny and Watcher glanced at each other. They were still on their first bottles.

"It is a bit," admitted Watcher.

"Doesn't worry us, though," said Dinny. "We're used to it."

"We thrive on it," added Watcher.

The men sipped their beer and talked about times when they'd had *really* crook beer. Leila finished cooking some lamb chops and eggs, offered again to get some for the men, and then sat down between them and ate her meal. By the time she'd finished they were almost visibly drooling. They drank determinedly on for a while, talking about perks, pubs, and deals they were working on. Nothing important in front of the girl, just everyday stuff.

Eventually Watcher said: "This is the worst beer they palmed off on us for years."

"You can say that again," said Dinny.

"Too fresh."

"They don't give it time to brew properly these days," agreed Dinny.

"All chemical beer. Not like the stuff we used to get."

"Spiggott's beer never travels well," said Dinny expertly. "Gets too shook-up. Takes weeks to settle properly."

"Yeah. We should have got something else."

"Of course we're out of condition. You have to take that into consideration ."

"Yeah. Normally we'd clean this lot up in one sitting."

"Is all your beer ruined?" asked Leila politely.

"Not exactly ruined," said Watcher, trying not to burp. "It'll probably come right when it's had a few days to settle and cool off."

"There's some wine there," said Leila. "Shall I get you some of that?"

"No thanks," said Dinny quickly.

"Doesn't mix with the beer," explained Watcher.

"Shall I make you some sandwiches?" she suggested. "Wouldn't hurt," said Dinny with exaggerated carelessness. And they ate sandwiches as fast as she could make them until they'd used all the bread in the house. Then they sat round the table twiddling their conversational thumbs.

"Who'd like a game of cards?" asked Leila.

There was a brief silence.

"Okay," said Dinny resignedly.

"Sure," agreed Watcher.

Leila ran off to her room to get the cards. Watcher and Dinny glanced at each other again and then at all the bottles of grog around the room.

"She bluffed us that time," said Dinny.

"We bluffed ourselves," corrected Watcher.

Leila returned with the cards and handed them to Dinny to shuffle. "Strip-Jack-Naked?" she suggested.

"Okay," said Watcher. "Long time since I played it though. How does it go again?"

"One for a Jack, two for a Queen, three for a King and four for an ace," said Dinny.

They went on playing Strip-Jack-Naked until half past one next morning.

Reorganisation

FIVE

Reorganisation

"We'll have to have an emergency conference," announced Watcher over Dinny's kitchen table.

"What's up?" asked Dinny.

"We're getting too many complaints about our filling. They don't mind tins and bottles and stuff, but there's too much paper in it. Makes too much of a mess."

"People wrap everything in paper these days," said Dinny. "There's nothing we can do about that."

"If we don't do something about it we're going to lose valuable contracts," said Watcher grimly. "They've already cancelled two loads the Potter crowd wanted on the Lawrence Street section, and two of the others have got contractors in to cover up our jobs. If this goes on we'll have to start taking some of our loads out to the Council tip, and you know how that cuts into our time."

"We could back-load a few loads of solid stuff from the tip to keep our quality up," suggested Dinny.

"Too much time and work involved. It'd all have to be hand-loaded. Besides, they'd start getting curious about us if we started taking stuff away from the tip."

"We can't risk that," said Dinny. "I wouldn't be surprised if they don't start looking into our activities as it is. We're getting too big to operate under cover any more."

"Yeah, you're right. Looks like we'll have to drop the filling side of things for the time being and concentrate on perks and — Shhh, here's Leila."

Leila came in with a basket of washing. "The old green washing machine does a faster job than the last one you brought home," she said. "But I still like the wringer on the one outside. Between the three of them . . . Good heavens! What's happened to you two? You look as though the end of the world has arrived."

She put her washing on the end of the table. "Aren't people putting enough perks in their rubbish lately?"

"No, there's always plenty of perks," said Watcher. "It's another branch of the business we're worried about."

"We'll just have to drop it altogether," said Dinny to Watcher.

"Going to be a bit tough after all the time and work we've put in building it up," said Watcher.

"What is it?" asked Leila curiously.

The two men glanced at each other. Watcher shrugged. "It's a lurk we've had going for a fair while," he explained. "Instead of taking our rubbish out to the Council tip we've been selling it for seven-and-six a load to people who want filling on their sections or big holes filled up. Saves us time and brings in a bit of spare cash."

"That's a good idea!" said Leila. "What's gone wrong with it? Aren't there any more holes or sections to fill up?"

"No, it's not that. We could get enough contracts to keep us going for years. But people are complaining about all the papers in our stuff. Odd one or two going crook about smells and dogs scattering bones and things like that, but it's the paper they're really down on. People want the filling but they're not prepared to put up with a bit of mess that goes with it."

"We can't afford to be investigated," said Dinny. "If Council gets on to us our whole organisation'll collapse."

"How do they get on at the Council tip then?" asked Leila. "You don't see paper blowing everywhere like it used to."

"That's different," said Watcher. "They burn everything out there."

"Then why don't you burn yours?"

"No, we couldn't...." Dinny and Watcher looked at each other.

"We could on the Potter job," said Watcher.

"And the one at Eastwood's," said Dinny.

"What about the Haddock Street job?"

"Have to ask them first, but the old girl in Seldon Road won't mind."

In their enthusiasm they'd forgotten about Leila, who contentedly went on folding her washing at the other end of the table.

A few days later Dinny was pulling at a heap of rubbish they'd just tipped off the truck while Watcher waited for him.

"Come on Dinny. That stuff's no good to us. Put a match to it and let's get out of here. I feel exposed."

"Thought I saw a bike-pedal with good rubbers on it in here," said Dinny.

"What the hell do you want pedal-rubbers for?"

"Somebody asked Leila for some the other day and she couldn't find any round the yard. Told me to keep a lookout for some."

Watcher went over to help Dinny free the old bicycle frame he was pulling at. They dragged it out and shook off some wire and paper that was caught on it.

"There y'are," said Dinny. "A whole set of perfectly good rubbers. We'll need a spanner to get 'em off though. Might as well take the whole thing home and let Leila tackle it. She's pretty good with a spanner. The frame might come in handy for something one day."

"Leila's doing quite a bit of business lately," observed Watcher. "She always seems to be picking up orders."

"Yep," said Dinny with a trace of pride. "She's got orders for things from half the women in Essentry Crescent. And some of the people have got the flashest homes in the district. Wonder if their husbands know they're getting stuff from us?"

"We're not branching out into the blackmail business," said Watcher, throwing the bicycle frame onto the back of the truck. "Come on or we'll miss the pub."

On a small dairy farm thirty miles from anywhere significant, on a wild slashing night in April, a tree was struck by lightning, six sheets of iron blew off the cowshed roof, and three heifer calves and Harry Taggitt were born. The calves, which bore broken-coloured testimony to the ingenuity of a neighbour's mongrel bull, appropriately enough called Houdini, were sent to the works, while Harry survived to inherit the dairy farm when he was thirty. He sold it as soon as it was his to sell. Then he invented an infallible betting system for racehorses and had never dared to look back. He rented Number 21 Essentry Crescent and paid off large lumps of back rent every time he had one of his big wins.

Harry would probably have made plenty of friends except for one thing: He thought and spoke of everything in terms of horse-racing, and spoke so badly that it made everybody impatient to get away from him. He seldom saw a racehorse from one year to the other, but anyone who didn't know what won the Auckland Cup from 1929 to 1965 was a bloody immigrant, as far as he was concerned. His only interest in a newspaper was the list of acceptances for the next race meeting.

Harry was the City Council pay clerk and had never embezzled a penny in his life. Everyone he met, whether he knew them or not, was greeted with: "Got a winner for Trentham, mate?" or "What's going to win the cup?", depending on the time of year. Harry loved women, every man-jack of them, regardless of their age or what they looked like, but his obsession with horse-racing rendered him eminently unmarriageable and he was unlikely to ever be nominated for the Matrimonial Stakes.

Dinny's yard, three houses along the street from his place, never worried Harry Taggitt particularly, though if he was pressed he was prepared to admit they "oughter put the 'obbles on 'im". He was "among the starters" in Mr Tweek's anti Dinny's-yard activities, but he was waiting for the odds to shorten and was always "off his oats" whenever it came to actually doing anything. Mr Tweek had had hopes at one time that Harry would be a valuable ally, since he worked for the same people as Dinny, but it never worked out.

The only time Mr Tweek had seriously asked Harry's opinion about what should be done, he suggested that Mr Tweek cover the field with Dinny and hope for a double. He'd drawn too far out to race against him. Mr Tweek never bothered to interpret Harry Taggitt's advice, or ask for it again. And yet it was Harry Taggitt who came nearer than anybody had yet managed to disrupting Dinny and Watcher's organisation.

Watcher arrived at Dinny's place for a conference and there on the kitchen table was what looked like a big rusty cage.

"What do you think of that?" said Dinny, proudly banging the top of the thing with his hand.

"What is it?"

"A meat-safe," said Dinny. "Leila made it up," he added, opening the door of it. "See? There's three safes, one inside the other." He opened the second door. "They've all got holes in them, but if flies do get into the outside one they'll be lucky to find the holes in the next one. And if they get into the second one," he opened the third door, "they'll be dead long before they ever find their way into the inside one!" he finished triumphantly.

"Er — yeah. Sure," blinked Watcher.

"I always knew them safes was worth hangin' on to," said Dinny.

"Yeah, well we'd better have a conference," said Watcher, remembering the purpose of his visit. "An emergency conference. The Council's on to us."

Dinny quickly put the safe on the floor and sat down.

"Hell," he said. "What happened? Someone complain?"

"No. When I was putting the scrapwaggon away just now old Archie gave me a message from Bilter. He wants to see both of us in his office before we start work in the morning. Harry Taggitt saw us parked on the Haddock Street job and Bilter heard him asking Archie what we were doing there. Don't let on we know that, or Archie'll cop it for telling us."

"It was bound to happen sooner or later," said Dinny. "We just got too big for them."

"We're not going to be too big if they give us the bullet," said Watcher. "Our whole organisation's based on the Council job."

"What are we going to do then?"

"Depends how much Bilter knows," said Watcher thoughtfully.

"We could tell him we were tipping the stuff off there to save mileage on the truck," suggested Dinny. "That might help."

"If they find out we've been selling the stuff, nothing'll help," said Watcher. "It could be theft, the way the law works."

"Who owns rubbish anyway? The people who throw it out or the ones who pick it up?"

"Never run into anything on the ownership of rubbish," admitted Watcher. "I've always thought it belonged to whoever picks it up first."

"That's not what they'll go us for anyway," said Dinny. "I can just hear old Bilter: using their truck, in their time, selling their refuse. Betraying the Council's trust in us. He'll most likely tear a few strips off us and let us off with a warning."

"Even if they did let us stay on they'd keep such a close watch on us it wouldn't be safe to keep on with any of our side-lines," said Watcher.

"Yeah. We'll be bloody lucky if they don't prosecute us."

Leila came in looking puffed with a big bag of groceries. She put them on the bench and flopped into a chair.

"Hello," she said, sweeping her hat off and shaking her hair. "Another conference? How's it going?"

"We've decided to leave the Council," said Watcher.

"But I thought you were both quite happy with your job?"

"We're happy enough," grunted Dinny, "but we're not so sure about the Council."

"They've unearthed our filling business," said Watcher.

"Oh. That's bad."

"It'll be worse than bad if they start investigating us," said Dinny. "There's no tellin' what they might dig up."

"Have they told you what they're going to do?"

"We've got to report to the boss in the morning," said Watcher. "We know for certain we'll probably get the sack over it at least."

"Yep, we're finished," said Dinny. "The whole organisation was built up around the Council job. Now it's finished we'll have to start all over again with something else. Eight years of back-breaking labour gone for nothing."

"But the Council job is only a small part of your work," protested Leila. "What about all the other things?"

"Can't work them without the old scrapwaggon," said Watcher. "Everything depended on that truck."

"Couldn't we get a truck of our own?"

"We'd need at least five hundred quid before we started," said Dinny.

"Then we'll get it," said Leila.

"Where would we get all our raw material from?" asked Dinny. "Even if we did get a truck?"

"Right here — the Council tip — demolition jobs," she said.

"There's rubbish all over the city, it's just a matter of looking for it."

"Be all right if we could swing it," said Watcher.

"There's probably two or three trucks out in the yard here," said Dinny. "It's just a matter of finding one and putting it all together."

"That'd take years," said Watcher absently. "What have we got that's worth five hundred quick quid?"

"Nothin'," said Dinny.

"If there's not five hundred pounds' worth of something somewhere in this yard," said Leila, "I'll be very surprised. What can we get a ready sale for? There must be something."

"Copper's worth forty quid a ton just now," said Dinny. "There's plenty of that around."

"White-metal, bronze, brass, lead — they're all fetching good prices," said Watcher. "But who's going to dig it all out?"

"Me," said Leila. "Just show me what it looks like and I'll start gathering it tomorrow. There's no telling what I might find."

"Please yourself," said Dinny. "I'll show you what to look for in the morning. But I still think you're wastin' your time."

"Nothing to lose," said Watcher. "We'll need every few bob's worth of perks we can get, by the looks of it." He stood up. "I think I'll go home. You'd better come round to my place early in the morning, Dinny. We'll go down and see what old Bilter's got up his sleeve. Goodnight, Leila."

"Goodnight, Mr Amble. And don't worry about it. Everything's going to work out all right. I'm sure of it."

"Goodnight."

Watcher was waiting at the corner of the road next morning when Dinny came hurrying along and fell into step beside him.

"Sorry I'm late," he puffed. "Not used to getting up this early.

And Leila held me up to explain about the scrap-metals. She's started fishing out stuff already."

"She's keen enough, I'll say that for her.'

"You never know what she might find," said Dinny. "I couldn't tell you what's in amongst all that stuff myself off hand. And you know how the demand for things keeps changin' all the time. Stuff that wasn't worth anything a few years back is practically priceless today. Worth quids, some of it."

"What sort of things?" asked Watcher absentmindedly.

"Can't think of any on the spur of the moment," said Dinny. "But there's perks in that yard of mine that've been unobtainable for years!"

"That's because it's *all* in your yard," said Watcher. "Here we are. Let's go in and get it over with."

Dinny stopped at the gateway of the Council Depot. "I think I'll let you go in and talk to him, Watcher. I'll just wait out here and you can tell me all about it later."

"Bilter wants to see both of us," Watcher reminded him.

"He might be satisfied with just one," said Dinny. "If he insists I'll be right here. You can give me a whistle."

"Okay, I'm going in to get it over with. Can't stand the suspense."

Dinny watched Watcher go into the office building and settled down to wait, half behind the gatepost. He was still far from settled when Watcher came out again and waved him round to the yard behind the building. Dinny caught him up in the driveway.

"What did he say?" he asked shakily.

"Week's notice," said Watcher. "Let's grab the waggon and go somewhere we can talk. Our Hale Road sub-depot'll do for a quick conference."

Watcher eventually pulled the truck into their Hale Road conference place and got out the survival kit. This was a real emergency.

75

"What's up?" demanded Dinny, grabbing the thermos. "What's this week's notice business? What did he say?"

"Just said that the pay clerk, Harry Taggitt, saw us parked on that place up in Haddock Street when we should have been over in Aspin Bay. Wanted to know what we had to say for ourselves."

"What did you tell him?"

"Told him we were thinking of buying the place," said Watcher, grabbing a turn at the thermos.

"What'd you say that for?"

"Couldn't think of anything else to say," said Watcher simply.

"Well, go on!"

"He said he'd had complaints about our dumping, too."

"Did he say who potted us?"

"Yeah. The caretaker and the 'dozer-driver out at the tip. Said we'd been disrupting the whole system by not putting the stuff where we were told to."

"But we haven't dumped a load at the tip for weeks!" said Dinny. "It must have been one of the other trucks. We've been framed!"

"Think I was going to tell Bilter that?"

"What did you tell him then?"

"Nothin'. I just stood there and waited for him to say something. Thought it might have been a trap. Then he said he was giving us both a week's notice. Told me to be sure and tell you."

"Thanks," said Dinny, taking the thermos. "So you don't think he knows about our side-lines?"

"No. If he did we wouldn't be here now, you can bet on that. I think he wanted me to start crawling around his office asking for our job back, but it's no good to us now anyway. The first time we made a blue they'd be on to us like a ton of rotten cabbages."

"Suppose you're right," said Dinny. "Let's get this run cleaned up. We should get enough fillin' in a week to finish off one or two of the small jobs."

"We're not giving any of our valuable filling to those blabbermouths out at the tip, after the way they've been talking about us behind our backs," said Watcher. "That's for sure."

They finished the Council run early in the afternoon. Then they did one of their own and decided to knock off. Watcher stopped the truck outside Dinny's place.

"Aren't you coming in?" asked Dinny. "I think Leila's expecting you for a feed."

"Not tonight, thanks," said Watcher. "Think I'll go home and have an early night. It's been a big day."

"Yeah, sure," said Dinny. "See you tomorrow."

Watcher was still trying to wake up next morning when Dinny arrived and burst into the hut.

"Quick. Get up. Come and see what Leila's done. I got the truck outside. You can eat over home. Wait till you see this!"

Watcher sat up in bed rubbing his face with his hands. "What time is it?"

"Wake up man," said Dinny. "Come and see what Leila's done."

"She find a truck yesterday?"

"No. Brass! Copper! Lead! Everything. She's got over half a ton already and she hasn't scratched the surface."

"Half a ton, eh?" said Watcher.

"Throw a pair of pants on and come and see for yourself."

Watcher got out of bed. "Half a ton," he mumbled.

"More," said Dinny. "Don't you see what that means?"

"No," said Watcher, looking under the bed for one of his socks.

"If Leila can get half a ton in a day, the three of us can get a ton and a half, easy. That's over fifty quid a day. I tell you she's hardly scratched the surface."

Watcher, knowing Dinny's enthusiasms as he did, didn't take this one any more seriously than he usually did — until they got to Dinny's yard and he saw for himself. Leila was already at work, digging around in a big heap of everything. She only stopped to say hello and then went on rummaging. At intervals along the path leading to the house, hitherto the only uncluttered area in the whole yard, were several large heaps.

"See this?" said Dinny, walking over to the heaps. "This is all brass — this is the copper — here's the white-metal, zinc, and lead. (A bit of aluminium mixed up with that lot.) And this is the stuff she's not sure about. We'll go through it later. How does it look?" he concluded.

Watcher was for the moment more stunned by the variety than the quantity or value. He was a perk-man himself, and over the years he'd become almost accustomed to Dinny's amazing yard. But this was as though everything he'd ever touched or seen had been gathered up and suddenly spread out in front of him.

There were brass taps and plugs and door-handles, bed-knobs, gongs, bolts, spikes, spokes, bells, brackets, wheels, window catches, hinges, switches, latches, locks, catches and clips.

There were copper fittings, connections, joints, nuts, disconnections, plates, unions, washers, attachments and teapots.

The white-metal, zinc and etceteras were lengths, widths, angles, shapes, sizes, depths, flats, rounds, squares, holes, concaves, convolutions, convexes and doovers.

The pile of miscellaneous was simply made up of pipes, weights, sheets, lumps, knots, blobs, balls, rolls, blocks, knobs, coils, hunks, bits and pieces.

This was just a first impression. Few men could have been confronted with all that at once and still believed in it.

"There's over half a ton there already," said Dinny proudly.

"Is that all?" said Watcher hypnotically.

"What do you think of it?" insisted Dinny. "We haven't scratched the surface yet, I tell you. You can see for yourself. Imagine what must still be in there!"

The idea was too much for Watcher.

"I think we'd better have a conference," he said.

So while Leila cooked them some breakfast Watcher and Dinny conferenced at the table.

"How much worth do you reckon you've got already?" asked Watcher.

"According to the weights and prices Father gave me it's about thirty-seven pounds' worth," said Leila. "I worked it out last night."

"At that rate we're really sitting on a fortune," said Watcher.

"It's pretty good where I'm working at the moment," said Leila. "But I've had a look at a few other places where there's hardly any of the stuff we want. I think we're going to find it mostly in pockets here and there."

"We'll get enough for a truck of our own, though," said Dinny.

"We don't need a truck or a business," said Watcher. "With a couple of days prospecting every week or two we could live off this yard for the rest of our lives and still leave enough to cover our death duties."

"No fear," said Dinny. "I'm making this sacrifice to get us on our feet. I don't like parting with me gear. It's taken me years to collect it all together. As it is I'll probably be left with hardly anything in the metal line but cast-iron."

"That's worth seven quid a ton," said Watcher.

"You're not selling off my good stuff indiscriminately, I tell you. It's got sentimental value."

"Now don't quarrel, you two," said Leila, putting plates of bacon and eggs in front of them. "It isn't going to be as easy as you seem to think. There's a lot of hard work to be done. Just because we had one good day doesn't mean it's all going to be like that. Most of the small stuff is buried under big heavy things and hard to get at. You'll have to help me shift it around."

"That's easy," said Dinny. "We'll hook a rope on to it and drag it clear with the truck. We can get a fair angle from out on the road."

"And are you sure we'll be able to sell it all?" she asked.

"Yep. That bloke in Haining Street'll take the lot. He's always coming round here trying to make me offers. No trouble there."

It was a busy week. Every morning one of the men collected the scrapwaggon as soon as the Council yards were open. By lunch time they'd have fulfilled their obligations to the Council and their clients. Then they used the truck in the afternoons to pull heavy objects clear of new places to prospect. Leila worked steadily away and the piles of scrap-metal grew until new finds had to be carefully placed on the heaps. If they were thrown they'd avalanche down the sides into the rubbish that surrounded them. To get to the house they had to climb and scramble. Groups of people constantly assembled and dispersed in the road outside, speculating hopelessly as to what exactly was going on in the yard of Number 17. Mr Tweek telephoned the Council and wrote letters.

Watcher and Dinny put in all the time they could helping Leila, but Dinny wasn't a very efficient prospector: he kept rediscovering things he hadn't seen for years and getting carried away with what Watcher described as nostalgia. He'd often get so mixed up in the past he'd forget what he was looking for. He was usually nominated to return the scrapwaggon to the depot when they'd finished with it in the afternoons.

On the day before their week's notice expired Dinny drove the truck in to the depot, parked it, turned in the keys, and was ambushed in the driveway by his almost ex-boss, Mr Bilter.

Norman Bilter was one of those people who are hard to imagine unless you're actually looking at them. And then there is no doubt about it. He devoted his working hours to writing reports to The Committee and working out what he was going to say to the next of his "chaps" he'd be obliged to reprimand. At home he had his wife. His favourite broadsides were "Betrayed Trust", "All One Big Happy Family Here", and "I'll Try To Keep This From The Committee But I Can't Guarantee Anything". He'd been a foreman on the City Council since before there was a City Council, and genuinely believed himself to be considered "a bit of a wag". He ambled around the corner of the office block and intercepted Dinny with disgracefully-acted surprise.

"Oh, Mr Virtue," he said. "I'm pleased I ran into you. I've been wanting to see you and Mr — e-r — Ambler.' Would you mind stepping into my office for a moment please?"

"I'm in a bit of a hurry," said Dinny doubtfully.

"I won't keep you a moment. I think you'll be interested in what I have to say to you."

In the office Mr Bilter sat behind his desk while Dinny stood against the wall to one side. Mr Bilter pulled his old trick of pretending to read a report to make his visitors nervous.

"If you're busy I'll drop in tomorrow," said Dinny nervously.

Mr Bilter lowered his report and suddenly noticed him.

"Oh yes," he remembered. "I wanted to see you about your week's notice. You and Mr — er — Ambler, isn't it?"

"It's up tomorrow," said Dinny.

"Yes, yes. I rather thought we might have received an explanatory report from you both. As a matter of fact I've left the matter rather open with The Committee in the hope of hearing from you." His words barked around the room like something trying desperately to escape.

"Yeah, well we'll think it over," said Dinny uncomfortably.

"You realise that in a case such as this, betrayal of the trust we've placed in you, we must be firm. However, Mr Godfrey reports that you have been first to arrive for work every morning this week. In view of this extra effort you are making, and your long service with us, we are prepared to reconsider our decision on the matter. I want to be fair about this, and I don't mind telling you that you and Mr — er — Ambler were thoroughly investigated. I must say I'm very pleased with the results." He smiled as though he'd just laid an egg, and sat back in his chair to remember what came next.

It wasn't the first straight-out lie Mr Bilter had told Dinny, but it had the same disconcerting effect.

"Beg your pardon?" he said.

The smile dropped off Mr Bilter's mouth as though he'd just broken his egg.

"What I'm saying is that if you can give us your assurance that nothing of this nature will happen again, we're prepared to let the matter drop. You and Mr — er — Ambler can continue with your duties, and no reference to this will be included in your employment files. I had to tell The Committee that I'd personally take the responsibility. But I've a great deal of faith in you chaps."

"I don't know if we will be able to stay with you," said Dinny uncomfortably. "We're going into business on our own account. I'd have to have a conference with my partner before we came to any decisions about work."

A similar look would have crossed Mr Bilter's face if someone had just whispered in his ear that the chairman of The Committee was carrying on with Mrs Bilter.

"I see," he grated warmly. "Congratulations. May I ask what kind of business you're going into?"

"We might be able to offer you a contract price for our present collection area," said Dinny.

"Well naturally such a proposal would have to be brought before The Committee," said Mr Bilter doubtfully.

"That's okay. Drop us a line and let's know what they reckon about it. I'll write my address down for you if you like," he offered.

"Well actually we didn't realise that you and Mr — er — Ambler would treat this so seriously," said Mr Bilter. For the first time in years he was lost for words, with the result that he was beginning to talk sense.

"A week's notice is a week's notice," pointed out Dinny.

"We — er — haven't taken any steps to replace you," said the new Mr Bilter.

"That's going to be awkward," said Dinny unsympathetically. "There's going to be a right old mess in the area if you don't get someone schooled up on it pretty soon. You can cut people's power off and increase the cost of living, anything you like. But if you don't collect their rubbish they really perform."

"Yes, yes. Quite. Perhaps you and Mr — er — Ambler might like to stay on and help us out until we can come to some arrangement," said the new Mr Bilter anxiously. "In fact I had this very thing in mind when I assured The Committee that you chaps would never let the Council down in an emergency," added the old one.

"I'll speak to my partner about it," said Dinny. "We'll let you know what we decide as soon as we can. I'd better get goin' before I miss me dinner. See you tomorrow." And he left the old Mr Bilter sitting in his office wondering what he was going to say to The Committee.

That night there was another conference at Dinny's place. He told Watcher and Leila as much as he could remember about his interview with Mr Bilter.

"Load off our mind," said Watcher. "Several loads, when you come to think of it. Bilter'll keep out of our hair, and we can use the scrapwaggon to cart our scrap in."

"How much do you reckon we've got ready to sell?" asked Dinny.

"Tons," said Leila. "We've put the lead into bags, there's about four hundredweight of it. But I'm afraid I've lost track of the other stuff. It's just too difficult to estimate."

"We'll have to cash in on it now anyhow," said Watcher. "No room for any more. It's leaking back into the other stuff as it is."

"Right," said Dinny. "I'll ring that dealer from the depot in the morning."

Non-ferrous

SIX

NON-FERROUS

Like most people who have nothing else to be, Ernest Looper was fiercely proud and prejudiced. His father had died of disappointment when Ernie was still a whimpering boy of nineteen, and his mother never forgave him for his voice dropping.

Ernie had never been able to look ahead, or back, but by looking sideways and trusting nobody he'd managed all right. At forty-five he'd worked his way up from the ground floor to the basement, and although his success owed itself almost entirely to other people's ignorance, his own was unimpaired. He was a self-made scoundrel.

The 'phone in his office rang. He let it ring six times before he snatched up the handpiece.

"Looper Metals. Looper speaking, what can I do for you?"

"Dinny Virtue here. We were wondering if you'd be interested in a load of brass."

"I think we might be able to help you, provided it's good brass. Where can we inspect it?"

"We'll bring a load over to your place this afternoon, if you like," said Dinny.

"I think I'll be in all afternoon," said Ernie. "I'll be happy to have a look at it and give you a quote."

"Right, see you then."

Dinny and Watcher finished their garbage-run by eleven-thirty that morning and they and Leila spent two hours loading most of the brass on to the scrapwaggon. Ernie Looper came out of his office as Dinny and Watcher drove into his yard with what looked like a load of trash.

"You can't come in here with that," he yelled angrily. "I don't want a mess in here."

"I rang up about a load of brass this morning," said Dinny. "We've got it under here."

"Is it stolen?" asked Ernie shrewdly.

"No, it's from my place."

"Hey, I know you. You've got that junk-yard up in Essentry Crescent. So you've decided to sell out, eh?"

"Have a look at this," said Watcher, pushing aside some of the trash that covered the load.

Ernie Looper had a look, and then another. He walked around the truck, pushing aside the trash here and there to look some more.

"What is it?" he asked.

"Can't you tell brass when you see it?" asked Dinny.

"Is this *all* brass?"

"Yeah," said Watcher. "All brass."

"We've got a bit more at home," said Dinny. "Couldn't bring it all in one load."

"I see," said Ernie sightlessly.

"Well do you want it or not?" asked Watcher.

"Oh yes, I'll take it. But I'll have to check it before I can give you a quote on it. . . . Not that I don't trust you," he added quickly. "It's just that we often get people coming in here with all sorts of things in mistake for brass."

"You tryin' to tell us we don't know our brass?" said Dinny indignantly.

Ernie glanced again into the back of the scrapwaggon. "Oh no," he said. "You know your brass all right."

They drove to the gasworks to put the truck over the weighbridge, then back to Ernie's yard to tip it off. He showed them where he wanted it tipped off and Dinny backed up the truck and raised the hoist. Ernie was a little stunned at the multi-voluminous vision of all that brass cascading on to the ground from the back of the scrapwaggon. He stumbled to his office and fetched a notebook and a ready reckoner and checked the tare weight painted on the side of the truck against the weighbridge note.

"Three ton, sixteen hundredweight and twenty-five pounds," he quoted.

"Thought the old waggon was groaning a bit coming up the hill there," grinned Watcher.

"We'll go back for the rest of the brass, if you like," offered Dinny.

"Yes, you do that," said Ernie, clutching his hands in front of him as though he was rubbing tobacco. "You could put it over the weighbridge on your way back to save time. In the meantime I'll start checking this lot."

The rest of the brass made up roughly half as much as the first load and took almost as long to throw onto the truck. Leila insisted on helping and was looking exhausted by the time they'd finished.

"You go and have a rest," Dinny told her. "You've been overdoin' it a bit lately."

"I'm all right, really," she said. "I'd like to come for the ride this time, if there's enough room for me."

"Sure," said Dinny. "You just take it easy while we throw these bags of lead on."

The two men loaded the bags of lead and got a cushion for Leila to sit on between them in the cab. After they'd got the weighbridge ticket Dinny drove back towards home.

"Hey," said Watcher, "you've taken the wrong turning back there. This isn't the way to Looper's."

"I think we'll just dump this lead off again before we take the brass in," said Dinny, turning into Essentry Crescent.

"But that'll make the load read four hundredweight more than we've got on," protested Watcher.

"That's right," agreed Dinny.

"That's cheating, and you know it," said Leila indignantly.

"I know Ernie Looper too," said Dinny. "I think we'll come out about even in the long run. You'll see."

Watcher and Leila sat in the truck while Dinny threw the bags of lead off the truck and dragged them back into the yard. Then he drove to Ernie Looper's yard in a disapproving silence.

Ernie was scratching around in a small pile of their last load when they backed up to the heap. Watcher handed him the weighbridge ticket and he checked it in his notebook.

"Twenty-six hundredweight, nineteen pounds," he said. "We'll make it twenty pounds," he added generously. "Let it go right there."

As he reached over to throw the hoist into gear Dinny caught a look from Leila that would have smelted all the brass they'd just cheated Ernie Looper out of.

"How much is all that worth?" he asked, climbing out of the truck.

"Well I can't check every bit of it," said Ernie reasonably, waving towards the pile of brass. "So I've weighed out a test hundredweight — here it is. Now look at this." He picked up several odd-sized lumps from beside the heap. "You can see for yourself; this is a bit of bronze and all the rest is cast-steel."

"It is too," agreed Dinny.

"It weighs just over five pounds," said Ernie. "I'll put it on the scales again and show you if you like."

"Take your word for it," said Watcher impatiently.

"I want to do the right thing by you on this," went on Ernie, "but if I lose five pounds on every hundredweight I'll do money on the deal. I don't have a very big margin on this kind of stuff, you know."

"What are you getting at?" asked Watcher. "Isn't the stuff good enough for you?"

"The bulk of it is," said Ernie quickly. "But I'm afraid I'll have to take five pounds off for every hundredweight. I have to protect myself."

The look Leila gave him would have smelted the whole load.

"We could load it all up again," suggested Watcher wearily.

"No, that's fair enough," said Dinny. "What's the lot worth at that?"

"I won't be able to tell you until I've had time to work it all out," said Ernie. "Do you want to wait?"

"No, she's right," said Dinny. "Just give us a receipt for it and we'll pick up the cash tomorrow."

"Right. I'll have a cheque ready for you by about half past eleven."

"Cash," said Dinny.

"Well, if you'd prefer cash," said Ernie uneasily. "It's a little more trouble, that's all."

"No trouble to us," said Dinny. "Would you be interested in a load of copper?"

"How much have you got?"

"About the same."

"Yes, I think I might be able to handle it for you," said Ernie helpfully. "Bring it in any time you like." And his ready reckoner closed like a hand on money.

As they drove out the gate Leila said: "Those things he showed us didn't come out of our brass, I know they didn't. He just put them in to cheat us out of our money."

"Crafty hunk of work, that one," said Watcher. "We'll have to watch him."

"He's not crafty," said Dinny. "He only thinks he is. If any dealer found five pounds of rubbish in a hundredweight he'd lop off at least ten pounds to make up for it."

"I was furious," said Leila. "I could have hit him on the head with his own piece of cast-steel."

"I can see that lead coming in mighty handy," said Watcher.

"Yeah," laughed Dinny. "While he thinks he's robbin' us he'll be happy enough to take everything we got. He's the only scrap-metal buyer in the city. But we'll come out pretty even on the deal."

Three days later they'd shifted all their scrap-metal to Ernie Looper's except for the lead, which they sold to the gasworks to establish a contact there. By insisting on being paid for each load before they dumped the next one, the only one they never got paid for was the last load of miscellaneous stuff. But they'd allowed for that.

On the day the project was completed Watcher and Dinny left the scrapwaggon at the depot, bought a carton of beer on their way past the pub and retired to Dinny's place for a conference.

"Have you noticed?" asked Watcher. "We haven't touched the grog for nearly two weeks."

"Hell, I'd forgotten all about it," said Dinny.

Leila put a bottle-opener and glasses on the table as soon as they came in.

"We're havin' a conference to work out how much money we've made," said Dinny.

"Four hundred and eighty-six pounds, fifteen," said Leila happily.

"Er — Yes. Well we'd still better have a conference to work out what we're going to do about it," said Watcher.

"The money's non-taxable, too," went on Leila. "It's a sale of assets. I checked up."

"We don't usually bother about taxes," said Dinny, pouring himself a drink. "They get a fair whack out of our Council wages as it is."

"We'll have to pay taxes if we're going into business. I'll do all that kind of thing anyway. You don't have to worry about it."

"Four hundred and eighty-six smackeroos," said Watcher. "And you can't even see where it came from," he added reverently.

"I can," said Dinny. "All that stuff was underneath the big gear. It doesn't show much on the outside, but it's eaten into me holdings. We've got to keep this yard stocked-up, you know. It's the backbone of our whole organisation."

"It's not an organisation," said Watcher, reaching for the bottle. "It's a bloody empire."

Leila suggested that now they were expanding they should get themselves an official name for the organisation. But the men disagreed on the grounds that if they started calling themselves fancy names people might begin to wonder why. So they stayed unofficial for the time being.

"We ought to get a policy and stick to it."

"Specialise in unusual stuff. We don't want to be competing with the army-surplus stores, second-hand dealers, Woolworths, and the Council Tip."

"What about the truck we're going to buy?"

"Don't need one as long as we've got the old scrapwaggon."

"We can use the money to speculate with. Build on it."

"We can be independent of the Council any time anything goes wrong now."

"But with a truck of your own you wouldn't have to be dodging the boss all the time."

"We're used to workin' that way now."

"That's half the fun of it," said Watcher. "But we'd better see Bilter pretty soon and find out what he's done about getting us a contract. He's had a week to talk it over with his committee."

"If you ask me he's goin' to try and stall us off," said Dinny. "Keep us on wages as long as he can. That's the impression I got anyway."

"We'd better bail him up tomorrow and find out exactly where we stand," said Watcher.

"You could drop in on him when you go for the waggon in the mornin'," said Dinny brightly.

"You always leave me to handle Bilter," protested Watcher. "We're both in this together, you know."

"But you're our public-relations expert," said Dinny flatteringly. "And besides, if the two of us get talkin' to him we might contradict each other and blow the whole works."

So Watcher knocked on the door of Mr Bilter's office next morning and waited the usual twenty seconds to be told to come in. Mr Bilter was pretending to be thoughtful over a report by screwing his face up, but it looked more as though he had something in one of his ears. Watcher closed the door behind him and waited patiently to be noticed.

"Ah, Mr — er — Ambler," said Bilter at last. "What can I do for you?"

"Dinny and I have been wondering when you're going to let us know about working on contract. We've been holding off our other arrangements for over a week now."

"Yes, yes. I see," said Mr Bilter uneasily.

Watcher saw at once that he was stalling. "We'd like to know where we stand with the Council," he said respectfully.

"Quite right. As a matter of fact I'm pleased you came in to see me this morning. I fully intended asking you to drop by."

"What's the verdict?"

"Verdict?" echoed Mr Bilter vaguely.

"What did the committee say about us offering to work on contract?" asked Watcher patiently.

"Oh, that."

The truth of the matter was that Mr Bilter had never reported the matter to The Committee in the first place. He'd only intended to reprimand the chaps for loafing on the job and throw a scare into them. He'd had no idea it was going to backfire like this. Watcher's visit shattered his hopes that everything might smooth itself out and the incident be forgotten. The consequences of his little bluff were becoming more serious all the time. Two of his oldest employees sacked for a minor breach of the regulations, no effort made to replace them, the pay clerk not notified, and no report made to The Committee. And there was a memo on Mr Bilter's desk from the chairman, informing him that owing to the present shortage of labour, no labourers were to be dismissed until the circumstances had been referred to The Committee.

It was perhaps inevitable that one day Mr Bilter would outwit himself but for Dinny and Watcher to have him over a dustbin like this was a very timely stroke of luck for them. It was outrageous to Mr Bilter.

"You realise that a proposal such as yours, which involves a change of policy, requires lengthy negotiation, Mr — er — Ambler," he blustered. "Before we can set such a precedent The Committee has to investigate every aspect of the matter very exhaustively."

At the mention of "investigation" Watcher had a bad moment, but Bilter forged ahead reassuringly: "I appreciate your desire to — er — better yourselves, but I can't stand by and let two of my best chaps enter into anything ill-advisedly. Why, I'd feel personally responsible if your venture were to fail because of an oversight on my part. My loyalty to The Committee and my high personal regard for you and Dinny places me in a very difficult position. I have to try and do the best I possibly can for both parties. I had to put forward some very convincing arguments to get this before The Committee in the first place," he confided blinkingly.

Mr Bilter's own verbal momentum was beginning to restore his confidence. He went on: "There was considerable opposition from some of The Committee members at first, but I'm glad to be able to tell you that I'm gradually swinging the balance. I don't mind telling you, Mr — er — Ambler, I'm staking my reputation and judgment against that of The Committee. That's how much faith I have in you and Dinny."

Mr Bilter knew from experience that if he kept it up long enough he'd have Watcher agreeing with him. Everybody had their breaking-point. He paused to assess the effect it was having on Watcher, who saw the opportunity and spoke:

"We're not all that interested in the refuse run," he said. "We'd like to have the contract, but we can get plenty of other work. We just want to know how we stand with the Council."

"But it's my duty," said Mr Bilter desperately.

An hour later Watcher got out of there, feeling as though he'd just spent a month in a Turkish bath. He collected the scrapwaggon and drove round to pick up Dinny.

"How did you get on with Mr Bilter?" asked Leila, greeting the exhausted Watcher at the door.

"You were there long enough," said Dinny.

"Don't know what's eating him," said Watcher, "but he seems to be desperate for us to stay on the job."

"What about the contract? What did he say about that?"

"Lost track of him in the finish. Far as I can make out there's nothing doing. Reckons he's still trying to swing it with his committee."

"He probably hasn't even told them about it," said Dinny.

"Looks to me like he might have been ticked off about giving us the sack in the first place," said Watcher. "We've been with the Council long enough."

"Do you think he knows something about our organisation and wants evidence to dob us in?" asked Dinny.

"No," said Watcher definitely. "If Bilter had anything on us he'd hit us with it. Wouldn't be able to resist it. Anyway he said we needn't take the waggon back to the yard every night. We can keep it here to save time and just shoot it in on Wednesday mornings to be serviced. Felt a bit sorry for him in the finish. Told him we'd stay on in the meantime."

"Keep the waggon out overnight?" said Dinny wonderingly. "That's sure something for old Bilter!"

"It wasn't his idea," said Watcher. "He pinched it from me."

"Well it suits us nicely," said Dinny. "Business as usual and we don't need to buy our own truck yet. I didn't like the idea of partin' with the old scrapwaggon. She's been a great asset to us."

"Never let us down yet," agreed Watcher.

"But you will be careful not to get into trouble, won't you," said Leila anxiously.

"Bet your life," said Watcher, following Dinny outside.

Made men

SEVEN
Made Men

Under the new system the organisation did a roaring trade. Dinny swapped two hundred and fifty glass insulators and a gallon of green printers' ink for three good go-kart wheels and one buckled one. Watcher found three-quarters of a beer carton of blue identification-rings for fowls' legs and Dinny sold them to three different poultry farmers for a net profit of twenty-eight bob. Then Leila sold a burnt-out 1½-horsepower electric motor out of the yard for ten bob. A dozen pocket-compasses Dinny bought off a dealer who wasn't keeping up-to-date on his prices for 15/6 each, sold for 17/6 to a rival dealer. Watcher found a drum of D.D.T. powder which he immediately sold for thirty bob. Then half a gross of gate-hinges cost Dinny a fiver on the deal. They made a clean-up by selling a dairy company back fifteen tallow-drums they'd thrown out two weeks before and couldn't get replacements for. They broke even on two prefabricated coffins and lost money on twenty-five axe-heads Dinny swapped for a quarter of a mile of grade-4 sandpaper with a manufacturing fault through it. A set of bar-stools were good, and five new pairs of trousers Watcher got off an old lady for a quid each — were stolen. Leila sold several more things from the yard and didn't tell Dinny. They got two more contracts for filling.

At the end of the month Leila figured out all the profits and losses and expenses in a special organisation book and announced a total profit of £35-15-6, but they could only find £28-10-9 of it, so they had to write the balance off as expenses.

"If this keeps up, we're made men, Watcher," said Dinny, reclining in the cab of the scrapwaggon. "There's no limit to what we can do, now we're on our feet financially. We'll probably have to rent another yard to take the overflow from the one at home before long. We can go round the factories and buy up all their flops — I've always wanted to do that. We could even put up a sign and advertise in the papers if we wanted to."

"We ought to do something for Leila," said Watcher. "That's what we ought to do. To show her how we appreciate all the work she's been putting into the organisation."

Dinny returned to earth from visions of himself in a limitless yard, inspecting the perks as his workers streamed in the gate with them.

"Too right," he said. "You're dead right. That girl's been a great asset to us."

"We'll get her something special," said Watcher. "A present."

"I know," said Dinny. "We'll make her an official presentation of the next real good perk we get."

"Cut it out," said Watcher. "She's surrounded by perks all the time."

"I'm not talking about second-hand perks that've been lying around the yard," snorted Dinny. "I mean a new one, straight off the scrapwaggon. We could even get a whole load of them and let her take her pick."

"Lay off it," said Watcher. "We're going to buy her a proper present out of a shop."

"Better quality in some of these perks than anything you'd buy in a shop these days," said Dinny. "I don't care what you say."

"We're still going to buy her something out of a shop," said Watcher. "Let's get this load dumped. We might have time to go into town and pick something out for her this afternoon if we get finished in time."

The choice of a presentation for Leila involved Watcher and Dinny, four different shops, and five different assistants, in a two-hour disagreement. It started with the choice of which shop to buy the present at. Dinny wanted first to try an auction mart, and then a conglomerated pawnshop. He eventually agreed to settle for a hardware store, and nothing less.

Then he wanted to get her a set of spanners, a range of cold chisels or a pair of gumboots. While Watcher was trying to get him to settle for a pair of tablecloths, the assistant walked away and left them, so they went to a department store instead.

The department store floorwalker and two of his assistants thought they were going to start fighting and escorted them stiffly off the premises. In a third store they finally agreed to settle for a book, and went off in search of a bookshop. Then the argument flared up again because Dinny wanted to buy a *Pictorial Engineering for Beginners*, and Watcher insisted on *Home Decorating for You*. They still hadn't reached agreement by closing-time.

"Why don't you each buy your friend a book?" suggested the taut assistant.

And that's what they did — neither showing the other what they'd bought. Then there was a short discussion on what cards to put in the books. The manager eventually made them take plain ones because he wanted to close the shop. They each then had to borrow his pen to write in secret on the cards. Then they found that the assistant had gone home and the manager had to make an angry job of gift-wrapping their books.

"Good thing we don't have to do this every day," said Watcher as they left the shop. "That bloke'd get on your nerves after a while."

"Bad-tempered lot of sods these shopkeepers," agreed Dinny.

Leila had their dinner ready for them when they slunk into the kitchen with their presents coming unwrapped in their hands.

"You're late tonight," she said. "Did you have a busy day?"

"We picked up a couple of things for you on our way home," said Watcher, shoving his present at her as though it was contagious.

Leila took the parcel and lifted the paper away from it.

"A book. How nice!" she said. "*Countries and Peoples Around the World*," she quoted from the cover.

The card fell out of the book and landed on the floor by Watcher's foot. He slid his foot over it but he was too slow. Leila had seen it.

"A card," she said bending down for it. "Let me see what's on it."

Watcher reluctantly took his foot away. Leila picked up the card and turned it towards the light. Watcher wondered miserably what the hell he'd bought that book for and why he'd written that on the card, and he cursed the manager of the shop for hurrying him.

"'For Leila, with love respects from Watcher'," Leila read from the card. "Oh Watcher, you dear old thing." And she kissed him hard on the face.

"I had the 'love' crossed out," he stammered. "Put it in by mistake."

"Oh go on with you," she laughed. "What's wrong with putting 'love' on a card, may I ask?"

Dinny had been fidgeting in the background all this time, and Watcher turned just in time to stop him sneaking off up the passage.

"Dinny's got something for you too," he said quickly. "Come on, Dinny. Give Leila her present."

It was the only time Watcher ever saw Dinny blush. Leila had to almost drag the book away from him.

"Am I allowed to ask what I've done to deserve all this?" she asked.

"Appreciation for helping the organisation," said Watcher.

"*Countries and Peoples Around the World*," read Leila from the cover of Dinny's book. "Oh you silly old things. You've both bought the same book. What happened?"

"We — er — we had a bit of a rough time working out what to get so we both bought something in the finish," said Watcher uncomfortably.

"How sweet of you," she said. "What's on the card?"

"Hell," was all Watcher could say. Dinny was beyond words. Leila read the card he'd put in the book. Watcher waited interestedly to hear what Dinny had written on his card.

"'Compliments of the Season'," read Leila. "'Yours Faithfully, D'."

She threw her arms round Dinny and kissed his horrified whiskery cheek.

"You funny old things," she said. "Fancy both buying the same book. I love you both."

Almost simultaneously Watcher and Dinny both reached into the cupboard for the wine bottle. Leila skipped around them laying the table, kissing them each on top of the head every time she went past.

"Oh, I've got a surprise for you too," she said. "I almost forgot. We're losing one of our neighbours."

Dinny immediately thought of the neighbour on his right as you face the road, who'd built a six-foot fence three years before and hadn't spoken to him since. But it was the neighbour on his left as you face the road who had triumphantly announced to Essentry Crescent at large that he'd finally sold his house, against the overwhelming odds of his next-door neighbours. It had been up for sale since 1957.

"Old Kirkwood won't be any loss as far as I'm concerned," said Dinny. "But it's not often they sell houses around here."

"Wonder who bought the place," said Watcher.

"We might get some nice neighbours," said Leila. "The ones we've got now hardly ever speak to you."

The man who'd bought the place next door with the idea of letting it had reason to regret the investment. He advertised with flagging optimism and lowering rental for two months before finding a tenant. The kind of people who usually lived in that kind of neighbourhood just weren't equal to the challenge of living next door to Dinny Virtue's yard.

Ashley Nash didn't ask to be born and his parents didn't mean him to be. His father rejoined the ship when Ashley was still on the breast, from which he was taken early. His mother was impatient for him to get his early life over and done with so she could carry on with her own, and in the rush forgot to tell him it wasn't his fault. Ashley obediently grew up into a strapping lad as quickly as he could, and at sixteen he left home with just enough education to bewilder him and a conviction that he owed the world an apology. The last of his self-confidence was dispersed by a crop of pimples when he was seventeen.

On a visit to the country when he was eighteen Ashley went on his first horseback ride. The horse bucked him off and accidently kicked him in the face. The healed result was a rugged, craggy, beat-up set of features that could only conceivably have belonged to a professional light-heavyweight boxer.

If he noticed the change in other people's attitude towards him he certainly had no idea what caused it. He didn't realise that his timorous smile could now be interpreted as nothing but an arrogant grin. The way he stood whenever he was talking to anyone, as though getting ready to run at the sound of a harsh word, was now nothing but the natural, ready-to-spring stance of a born fighting man. The way he always moved around, as though he was being watched or followed, had become a bold swagger. Nobody with a face like that could ever skulk. His reluctance to meet people; his inability to look anyone in the eye; his unwilling handshake; his fear of opening his mouth in case he said something foolish — all these nervous mannerisms were automatically and unanimously misconstrued as part of the strong, silent, laconic, explosive nature of the man he looked. It was simply impossible to imagine anyone with a face like that being any other way. Even his name had a new menacing ring to it.

When he was nineteen Ashley discovered with a shock that other people were the same as him, and with the new confidence this knowledge gave him he began to enjoy life a little.

When he was twenty Ashley Nash had his one experience with love. He was spending his Christmas holidays at Waikaremoana and on the fifth day he was there he decided to explore a narrow, overgrown track that cut sharply up the side of a steep bush-covered ridge. He was toiling along, about halfway to the top, wondering how long it had been since the path was last trodden, when he suddenly saw a girl coming down the track towards him.

It might have been the unexpectedness of it, or the remoteness, or the time of year, or the fern — anyhow, whatever it was, it was love at first sight for Ashley. He'd never seen this girl in his life before, but he fell irretrievably in love with her right there and then. In a daze he watched as she floated gracefully down the path towards him. As she drew level she smiled and said: "Excuse me".

With his manners done up to the very top button, Ashley stepped politely back over the edge of the track and went plunging and rolling and crashing down the almost vertical hillside through the undergrowth. He finally landed with a jarring slosh in a shallow muddy creek two hundred feet below.

It might have been the shock, or the way he crashed down

through the bush, or the sound of the girl's voice, but whatever it was, by the time he'd climbed back up to the track Ashley had fallen out of love again. He never saw her again anyway.

When he was twenty Ashley was boarding with a family who didn't really want him there, working in the Meteorological Office and dreaming all day of inventions. He'd always had a flair for inventing things, but it was only now that he really started exercising it. And once he got started he really churned them out. Only all his discoveries had always been discovered before by someone else. He rediscovered things by the dozen, from indoor aerials and folding tables to slotted needles for mending fishing-nets. He found again for us such things as the polythene glasshouse, the patent gas-lighter, the gin-trap, a machine for painting the white line up the middle of roads, wallboard, snowshoes, putting your head between your knees to stop you feeling sick, the ramset-gun and the granny-knot.

Once he came close to striking something really valuable. Ashley had always been interested in glue and sticking things together. He wouldn't use a nail unless he absolutely had to, or a screw. Apart from having re-invented the dovetail joint he wasn't interested in joinery, or pegging or bolting or binding. But if two things could possibly be stuck together with glue, he'd mix up the right glue and stick 'em so stuck there was no getting them apart again without smashing them. And one day when he was experimenting around with different glues he found a combination that would stick glass on to rubber, or rubber on to rubber, or glass on to glass, instantly — and under water!

But nobody was interested in manufacturing patching-outfits for divers and he eventually gave up looking in the papers for something his glue could be used for.

But Ashley Nash didn't give up inventing, no sir! He went on turning out his rediscoveries at the rate of about half a dozen a week, and it was pretty certain that if he stuck with it he'd sooner or later come up with something that hadn't already been invented. If the wheel hadn't been discovered before then, it would never have got past Ashley. However, a detergent he invented which ate holes in the plumbing system of the house finally gave his landlady the courage to tell him to get out.

We make no excuses for the coincidence that Ashley Nash's new address was Number 15 Essentry Crescent, right next door to Dinny Virtue's place. If it hadn't been him it would have been someone else. The place couldn't stay empty forever, in spite of the neighbours. There's a housing shortage.

And it bears recording that, while the average citizen recoiled in varying degrees of shock at the sight of Dinny Virtue's yard, Ashley Nash was absolutely fascinated by it. It was an inventor's paradise.

"There's a man living in Number 15," said Leila excitedly, when Dinny and Watcher came in for dinner one night.

"On his own?" asked Dinny interestedly.

"He's the only one I've seen."

"How long has he been there?"

"I couldn't say. This morning was the first time I saw him. He came out and went off towards the bus stop this morning and came back just a little while ago. I passed him in the street on my way to the shop."

"Did you speak to 'im?" asked Dinny.

"Yes, I said hello, but he just put his head down and went past. I don't think he was being rude, though. He seemed very nervous."

"What's he look like?" asked Watcher.

"James Michener," said Leila without hesitation.

"If he's anything like the rest of 'em who live round here he won't be too nervous to start complaining about the stuff in me yard," said Dinny. "Blockin' his view, fallin' into his fence, blowin' into his garden. It always takes 'em a few months to find out we're not to be complained at. Old Tweek still thinks he's goin' to get the wood on me one of these days. He's been tryin' to get me out ever since I came here. I'll bet anything you like he gets on to this new bloke and tries to put 'im against us."

With the arrival of a new resident in the house next door to Dinny's yard, Mr Tweek's hopes soared to new heights. No one would voluntarily go and live in a position like that unless they had a very good reason. And no one had seen any furniture go into the house, or the man himself. He'd just appeared. He was probably a detective, getting evidence on Dinny for the new owner of Number 15.

Mr Tweek watched the newcomer very closely for two days, and then decided that his first guess had been right. There was no mistaking the watchful stealthy figure that strolled past two or three times a day, loitering casually past Dinny's yard. Mr Tweek hadn't spent forty years in uniform without being able to pick a plain-clothes man when he saw one. In fact it had always surprised Mr Tweek that they looked so obvious. Then one day as he watched the detective walking past the yard peering furtively over the fence, the woman that man Virtue was living with came out of the house. As soon as he saw her the detective spun round and walked quickly back to Number 15 and vanished inside. He'd been right all along. The man *was* a detective! Mr Tweek waited impatiently to see what he was going to do.

But he didn't do anything for a whole week, and Mr Tweek decided to take action himself. He was going to offer assistance to the detective. After all, nobody alive knew as much about this case as ex-Officer Tweek. At dusk he called on ex-Sergeant-

Major Fulton, who lived just along the street in Number 30.

Sergeant-Major Fulton (ret.) was perhaps the nearest thing to a friend or ally Mr Tweek had. Being an ex-army man, his regimented existence and his bellowing uncamouflaged voice rendered him unapproachable to anyone but collectors for charity, the wine-and-spirit merchant, Mr Tweek, the dachshund bitch two houses along, and anyone he could corner. He was a big man with small red, white, and blue eyes. His flesh had a soggy appearance as though it had been boiled along with his shirts and he peddled his frayed personality up and down Essentry Crescent in search of someone who could stand him.

He professed to share Mr Tweek's strong feelings about Dinny Virtue's yard, but apart from calling Dinny a "scrimshanker" and prescribing a spell in his regiment twenty years ago for him, ex-Sergeant-Major Fulton's only qualification as a supporter of Mr Tweek's cause was that he'd listened to so much of it he'd become committed.

Mr Tweek told the ex-Sergeant-Major of his discovery about the new chap in Number 15 being a detective and his plan to offer help. Ex-Sergeant-Major Fulton agreed to accompany him because he was too cowardly to refuse.

These two retired public servants lugged their sense of duty furtively across to Number 15 and knocked discreetly on the front door with it. After a short wait the door opened and the mendacious features of Ashley Nash peeped out.

"Good evening," said Mr Tweek. "I'm Officer Tweek, and this is Sergeant-Major Fulton. Both retired," he added.

"Yes?" asked Ashley apprehensively.

"We won't ask you your name," said Mr Tweek understandingly. "We understand how it is with you boys. We'd just like to have a word or two with you if you can spare the time."

Ashley slipped out through the door and closed it behind him.

Except for three blankets and a rickety chair he'd lifted over the fence from the yard next door the night before, the house was completely unfurnished. He couldn't possibly invite anyone inside.

"Don't worry about your equipment," said Mr Tweek shrewdly. "We won't give anything away."

"What equipment?" asked Ashley, his mind flashing guiltily to the incriminating chair.

"Your tape-recorders and things," said Mr Tweek, gesturing knowingly towards the closed door. "I used to be a detective of sorts myself, as a matter of fact. You don't have to explain to me."

"I — I don't know what you're talking about," stammered Ashley.

"Perhaps we'd better explain to the feller," rumbled ex-Sergeant-Major Fulton.

"Yes," agreed Mr Tweek. "You see we both live in this street. As a matter of fact I live directly opposite Number 17 here — That mean anything to you? — No? Well, I've been here for nine years, and the Sergeant-Major has been here for three years."

"I've only just arrived here," said Ashley politely.

"We know exactly why you're here, of course," said Mr Tweek, "and we think we might be able to help you with your investigations."

"I think you've come to the wrong place," said Ashley. "I don't know about any investigations."

Mr Tweek began to look a little disturbed. If he *had* made a mistake, and the Sergeant-Major told anybody . . .

"This blighter next door here," said ex-Sergeant-Major Fulton, waving towards where Dinny's junk loomed in grotesque silhouette above the fence. "How do you feel about this — er — rubbish of his?"

"I haven't thought about it," said Ashley nervously.

"But you're living right here beside it," protested Mr Tweek. "Closer than any of us. You must know how it feels to have it staring you in the face every time you look out."

"I don't notice it much," lied Ashley.

"Come now, old chap," grunted ex-Sergeant-Major Fulton. "We're only here to try and help you, you know."

"Yes," said Mr Tweek earnestly. "Everybody in this street will be right behind you."

"What for?" asked Ashley.

"To help you get this man and his disgraceful rubbish out of this street, once and for all. Make it fit for decent people to live in again. Free from ugliness and disease."

"But I've never met him," said Ashley. "What would I want to get him out of here for?"

"It's the junk in the yard that's the worst," said Mr Tweek shakily. "We all have to work in together if we're going to have any success."

"Oh I don't mind the junk," said Ashley. "In fact I saw some things I wouldn't mind buying, if the man wants to sell them."

Mr Tweek and ex-Sergeant-Major Fulton went home.

"He could still be a detective," said Mr Tweek haughtily, as ex-Sergeant-Major Fulton stopped at his house.

"Didn't say he wasn't," barked the ex-Sergeant-Major. "Didn't say he wasn't." And he closed his garden gate on Mr Tweek's next remark:

"Well I'm going to watch him very closely from now on. There's something very odd about that fellow, and I'm going to find out what it is. But I'm almost certain he's a detective all the same."

Mr Tweek watched Ashley come and go along Essentry Crescent, and the more he watched the more convinced he became that he was a detective, here to get evidence on Dinny

Virtue. He'd worked with the police and C.I.B. often enough to know a detective when he saw one. He was finally so certain that he decided to stand by and be ready to help if he was needed in any way.

Mr Tweek was still standing by the night Ashley walked the whole horrified length of Essentry Crescent with a nanny-goat trotting along beside him on a chain. It was snatching mouthfuls of flowers and hedges as they passed them. While Ashley waited for a car to pass before he crossed the road, the goat made a mess on the footpath right outside Mr Tweek's place. Ashley led the goat across to Number 15 and tied its chain to a tree in the front lawn, in plain view of the whole street.

Mr Tweek snatched up the telephone and dialled a number he knew by heart. This was going to be nipped in the bud, and he knew just the by-law to lodge the complaint under. There was no answer to his ring and he suddenly realised it was after six o'clock. He looked up the home number of the only councillor who hadn't been rude to him about his complaints in the past and dialled it.

The councillor's wife answered and offered to fetch the councillor from his dinner if it was urgent. It was, Mr Tweek informed her.

The councillor was quite curt when Mr Tweek identified himself, and then lost his temper completely when he heard what he'd rung up about. He called Mr Tweek such unpleasant and uncalled-for names that Mr Tweek had to break the connection.

He wasn't going to let *this* go unreported. He'd been abused over the telephone in filthy language by a city councillor for doing his duty as a law-abiding citizen. He dialled the number of the police-station watch-house. This was going to raise some action. It did. The telephone conversation with the constable at the watch-house was even more succinct than that with the councillor.

Ashley patted his goat and went inside to eat his fish and chips before they got cold. He'd always wanted an animal of his own.

"The man next door brought a goat home," said Leila excitedly. "A pretty little brown and white one."

"Wonder where he got it from?" said Watcher.

"Could be a good perk," said Dinny. "He ought to be able to sell it without much trouble. Never thought about dealin' in animals."

"Might want to just keep it for a pet," said Watcher.

"He brought it home on a chain," said Leila. "It's tied up on the front lawn, eating one of those little trees Mr Kirkwood was so proud of."

"That bloke might turn out all right, after all," said Dinny.

"A goat!" exploded ex-Sergeant-Major Fulton. "The audacity of the feller! The blighter can't be allowed to get away with it. This will have to be reported."

"I've already reported it," said Mr Tweek, "but I think perhaps if you yourself lodged a complaint tomorrow it would lend added weight to mine."

"I'll certainly do that," roared ex-Sergeant-Major Fulton, with no intention whatsoever of doing it. "I'm going to demand action on this, by George. What does that scrimshanking Virtue think we have here, a confounded menagerie?"

"Sergeant-Major — I'd appreciate it if you'd keep my little mistake about that chap being a detective just between ourselves," said Mr Tweek awkwardly. "If it were to get round it wouldn't help our complaints get a proper hearing."

"Confound it, man," boomed the ex-Sergeant-Major, "you're not suggesting that I'm one of those — gossip-mongers, are you? I don't go round spreading stories. More to do with my time. Can't answer for the feller himself, though," he added.

"We didn't actually *tell* him we thought he was a detective," said Mr Tweek.

"Well you did all the talking, Tweek. I hardly spoke to the feller."

"We could always say we were just checking up on him," said Mr Tweek uncertainly. "That's if he does say anything about it. We *were* checking up on him anyway, weren't we?"

"Of course, old chap. Naturally," said ex-Sergeant-Major Fulton reassuringly. "Absolutely nothing for you to worry about. I'd put it right out of my mind, if I were you."

Felicitations

EIGHT
Felicitations

Felicity Cambert was born to her parents in the nineteenth year of their marriage, when they were both in their early forties. The delighted couple gave her everything that was available, including discipline. Although she was their only child, they were determined that she shouldn't be spoiled, one way or the other.

They had her immunised against all the immunisable diseases and saw that her diet was balanced — but she wasn't made to eat anything she didn't like. She was encouraged to mix with other children and bring them home to play — as long as she asked first. They answered all her questions — as factually as they could. They had braces put on her teeth and let her wear her hair in whatever the prevailing fashion happened to be at the time for youngsters of her age. Her preferences were always courteously listened to and considered, and her misbehaviour punished firmly and fairly.

They provided her with a pony — which she could ride or not as she chose. They bought all the recommended books for the various stages of her development so that she could read them — if she felt like it. They bought a violin for her to try out, and hired a piano teacher to see if she preferred the piano. She went to dancing-classes of her own accord and also briefly attended a school of elegance for young ladies.

She grew up in the pleasant atmosphere of the big new rambling house on her father's 150-acre stud farm, half an hour's drive from the city. And she was educated at two tastefully chosen schools.

Felicity emerged from adolescence as an immunised, obedient, healthy, handsome, well-read young woman. She could dance, read music, ride, drive, and elocute.

On the other hand she was sloppy, bit her fingernails, and had no sense of rhythm or taste. And she seemed to have been immunised against education by mistake. So Mr and Mrs Cambert were pretty well back where they had started. The sole fruit of their otherwise happy union, and their combined and well-informed efforts to nurse it to maturity, was a twenty-one-year-old extrovert with a mind like a tennis racquet, who still had to be reminded when to take a bath. She was presentable enough, if you were quick, but the odds against her securing a passable husband were overwhelming. She was no more interested in men than she was in everything else. She could do nothing useful enough well enough to enable her to make her own living, and her weary parents gazed wistfully across rooms and tables at her, wondering where they went wrong.

Felicity herself was quite content to carry on as she always had done. She knew that she wasn't particularly useful or ornamental, but she wasn't sensitive enough for it to worry her unduly. She displayed only a perfunctory interest in the subject of young men when more or less told to do so by her mother.

When Felicity was a slightly stupefied but contented young woman of twenty-four, her father, who was now in his late sixties, decided to play the last card in what had started out as a full hand.

In spite of her assuring them that she'd just as soon stay home, they packed her off on her own on an expensive round-the-world tour. Then they sat back with their fingers crossed.

She returned unscathed. Without souvenirs, postcards, foreign words, answering any of their letters, a suntan, duty-free cigarettes, or impressions. She hadn't even been homesick, had trouble with customs and passports, or lost her purse in Cairo. She wasn't pregnant, and she couldn't remember the name of the ship she travelled on. Her six months abroad had made no difference to anyone, not even her fellow travellers. As she had told her parents before she left, she might just as well have stayed home.

She settled back in at home and contentedly looked after her mother, who was now a frail, wispy, sixty-six years old. She fetched and fussed happily about the house, helping anyone who wanted help, from the cook to the nurse who was pretending to cure her mother of old age.

In spite of her mother's poor health, it was her father who died first. The farm manager found him lying out in the paddock one sunny afternoon. Felicity was very sad at the loss of her father. She tried very hard to cry, but couldn't quite make it.

The nurse held off her mother's old age for eighteen months after that.

The first thing Felicity did on finding herself the owner of the estate was to sack the middle-aged farm manager because of something that happened twenty-two years before on a heap of superphosphate bags in the implement shed. Then she got the solicitors to hire another manager and put the place up for sale. She had sufficient brains to realise she wasn't equipped with enough of them to cope with the responsibility of making decisions involving 115 head of pedigreed stock, 150 acres of high-pressure pasture, three employees, two houses, and an annual turnover of around £12,000 a year. It was all she could manage to sign the deeds and transfers and things.

She was robbed handsomely by the buyer of the estate, and then by her own agent. Then the solicitor thought he might as well have a whack. She bought a house in town because at thirty-seven years of age she found herself a wealthy woman who knew nothing but how to live in a house. She was handsomely robbed on that deal too. She moved into Number 34 Essentry Crescent, with an elderly couple, who'd been with the family for ten years, to clean up after her.

Felicity Cambert also saw Ashley Nash lead his nanny-goat along the street and tie it up in what she still thought of as Mr Kirkwood's lawn. She saw most of what went on in the street from her front-room window. From one angle she could even see part of Dinny Virtue's fabulous yard. She'd have given anything for a yard like that. . . .

She turned from the window at the sound of someone knocking at the door, and heard her housemaid go to answer it. And ex-Sergeant-Major Fulton entered the room. He'd been calling in almost every day lately. Felicity thought he must be lonely and was vaguely sorry for him. She'd never been lonely herself, but she could imagine what it must be like.

"I say, have you heard about that blighter who's moved into Kirkwood's old place, m'dear?" began ex-Sergeant-Major Fulton harassedly.

"Into Kirkwood's old place?"

She'd discovered this conversational gimmick years ago, and for ex-Sergeant-Major Fulton it was just perfect. She simply had to repeat three or four key words of his last statement each time it was her turn to speak, and he'd go on for hours, doing all the thinking for both of them. All she had to do was sit back and listen. There were no noisy arguments and he was quite convinced that Felicity Cambert was a brilliant conversationalist.

"Yes m'dear," he said, plunging himself into the chair he always sat in. "It seems he's gone and brought a confounded goat into the street."

"A goat into the street?" she repeated with a trace of astonishment.

"Yes m'dear. Heaven knows where it's all going to finish up, what with that fellow Virtue and his great heap of scraps, and now this johnny bringing this wretched animal here. Tweek wants to report it to the authorities, but I've told him to hold his fire. He's done enough damage already lately, without going off half-cocked on this thing. He's too quick off the mark, old Tweek. Too quick off the mark altogether."

"Yes, too quick off the mark," agreed Felicity.

"Oh, so you've heard about him dragging me over there the other night to confront this chap with some evidence he'd got hold of? He thought the fellow was some kind of detective, spying on someone in the street. Tweek refused to tell me who it was. Confound the man, he's made me damnably curious. In any case he was quite wrong about this chap. Can't blame the fellow for getting a little hot under the collar really. Got to put yourself in his place — woken up in the middle of the night by an absolute stranger and confronted with some unsupported frumpery about being a spy. Reminded me of Austria during the war, with the Gestapo. Fortunately I was on hand to prevent it from developing into anything unpleasant."

"It's fortunate that you were on hand, all right," said Felicity.

"Yes," agreed the ex-Sergeant-Major with himself. "I managed to get things smoothed out between them in the finish. I must say, though, the feller would have been perfectly within his rights to take disciplinary action with Tweek."

"Quite within his rights," echoed Felicity.

"Yes," he went on, "a nasty-looking customer, when he's aroused, too, m'dear. Wouldn't surprise me if he was a prize-fighter with a circus, or something of that kind. I've mixed with that type quite a lot overseas, y'know. Nasty bunch. If this chappy had attempted to assault Tweek I would have been forced to use the old judo on him. Can't take risks with people like that, have to get them on the ground before they hurt someone. Wouldn't have liked to have to do it though; the feller had every right to order us off the property."

"Every right," agreed Felicity, squirming in her chair.

"But it still doesn't give the blighter the right to go bringing this confounded goat into the street. I must say I'm in full agreement with Tw — " The ex-Sergeant-Major's voice was choked off in his throat as Felicity rubbed her nose on the back of her hand, sniffed and swallowed noisily.

Now it may be true that ex-Sergeant-Major Fulton was a chronic gossip-monger. He might even be described as indiscreet. It might even be true that the big brass anti-aircraft shell standing to attention by his front door at Number 30 Essentry Crescent *did* come from Dinny Virtue's yard one night. It might be true, too, that ex-Sergeant-Major Oliver Fulton's discharge papers hinted at something unpleasant surrounding his departure from Her Majesty's Service. But whether these things were true or not, the one thing above all that he was scrupulous about was cleanliness. It was as though all his scruples had been channelled into this one thing. He couldn't abide filth, or even dirt. Untidiness made him uncomfortable, dust made him fidgety, and mud caused him to squirm, but this kind of thing was absolutely unbearable. The last time he'd visited Felicity she had stopped to scratch her back against the doorway of the sitting-room with a cup of tea in each hand, slopping tea into his saucer. The time before that he'd been unable to keep up his end of the conversation because she'd started scratching herself in all sorts of disconcerting places. Another time he'd had to leave early because she took off her slipper and rubbed between her toes with her thumb.

Rather than hurt the lady's feelings ex-Sergeant-Major Fulton had borne all these stomach-churning incidents with hearty stoicism, but the revolting thing he had just witnessed — the sniffing — was more than his delicate constitution could withstand. If he hadn't picked up the faint whiff of big money in the propinquity of Felicity Cambert he'd have got up right there and then and walked out. Things being as they were he gritted his back teeth, smiled with his front ones and forgot what he'd been saying.

"You've forgotten what you were going to say, haven't you," smiled Felicity. "I'm always doing that."

"No, m'dear," he said in his most avuncular manner. "I'm afraid you're wrong this time. As a matter of fact it suddenly occurred to me that every time I visit you the conversation always turns towards things like that fellow Virtue's latest activities, or someone else in the street here. You never mention your past life. It crossed my mind that perhaps you had some unpleasant — er — thing in your past you don't care to — er — talk about."

"No one ever asks me about it," said Felicity.

"Yes yes yes," said the ex-Sergeant-Major. "Of course one doesn't like to pry into the private affairs of one's friends, m'dear. But I have been concerned that a delightful young lady such as yourself should be shut away from the world like this. I had thought that possibly . . ."

He forgot what he was going to say that time because Felicity had just screwed her little finger into her ear and was revolving it around with a long-time-ago look on her face. But she had been listening.

"Don't be silly," she laughed. "I've always lived like this. I like living in houses, I've always done it, ever since I was a little girl."

"Of course, m'dear. Quite right." Ex-Sergeant-Major Fulton rallied his conversational troops. "Are your father and mother still with us, m'dear?"

"With us?" she asked.

"Er, alive," he said quickly.

"Oh no, they're both dead," said Felicity. "That's why I had to sell the farm and come to live here."

"Farming folk, eh!" he said jovially. "By George, isn't that a coincidence now? I was born and bred on the land myself, boy and man, until the old call came and I was needed overseas to help keep old Jerry off French soil . . ." He broke down again as Felicity began to squirm noisily in her chair again.

"I had to sell our farm," she said. "I couldn't look after it all on my own."

"No brothers or sisters, m'dear?"

"No. Just me."

"It must be very difficult for you, m'dear. As a matter of fact I dislike to discuss mercenary matters, especially with my friends, but any time you need help of a financial nature, m'dear, please don't hesitate to consult me about it. As a matter of fact I became so tired of all this money nonsense a few years back that I got all my capital together and hit the stock exchange. Made enough to retire on in comfort for the rest of my life. Made a little too much, as a matter of fact. I used a system an old soldier told me just before he died in my arms."

"Just before he died in your arms?" exclaimed Felicity.

"Yes, m'dear. Rather not go into that, if you don't mind. Yes, I used a selling and buying system that old soldier told me about and now I've got quite a tidy little pile invested here and there. More than I'll ever be able to use, so if you should ever need a few hundred pounds . . ."

"How much did you get?" asked Felicity interestedly.

"Well, I've never been able to get the exact figures," said ex-Sergeant-Major Fulton. "Changing values and rates of exchange and all that y'know. Well over a hundred thousand, I should say."

"I didn't get mine off a soldier," said Felicity. "It's just the money I got for the farm."

"How much did you get for your farm, m'dear? Perhaps if it

were handled sensibly it would be enough to keep you independent for a good many years."

"I don't know how much there is left," said Felicity. "It's all in Mr Stalker's bank."

"The things you women do with your money," laughed the ex-Sergeant-Major. "All your eggs in one basket. Haven't you ever heard of a run on a bank?"

"I think so. What does it mean?" asked Felicity doubtfully.

"They always keep it pretty quiet, m'dear, but sometimes a bank goes bung, just like any other business. It's all very complicated . . .." There was a longish pause. ". . . I — I'm afraid I haven't time to explain it to you just now. I'll have to be going. 'Bye now."

That longish pause and the ex-Sergeant-Major's sudden departure was because Felicity had suddenly poked out her rolled up tongue and coughed wetly, straight into his face.

From behind her curtain Felicity watched him hurry down the footpath to his place and smiled mischievously. She knew she shouldn't really do things like that to the poor ex-Sergeant Major, but it was such fun watching him squirm, and he was such a terrible bore.

Establishing neighbourly relations with Ashley Nash was not a simple thing to accomplish. Once Watcher waved to him and another time Dinny called out "G'day", but he pretended not to see or hear and scuttled for cover. They might have put him down as a crank and forgotten about him, but Leila had actually spoken to him in the store and reported that he was "a very nice man". So they went on being prepared to like him if they got the chance.

The nanny-goat had stripped fifteen years from the departed Mr Kirkwood's shrubbery and started on the hedges by the time

Dinny and Watcher got to meet their new neighbour, and then it was more or less a chance encounter. Dinny, clambering reminiscently through the hills and valleys of his estate one Saturday afternoon, was surprised to observe a backside sticking out of a heap of old beehive frames and bent tubular scaffolding. The backside was that of the elusive Ashley Nash.

"G'day," said Dinny pleasantly. "Can I help you?"

At first Ashley wouldn't come out. And when he did he just stood there in speechless embarrassment.

"You're the bloke from next door here, aren't you?" asked Dinny to start the conversation.

"Yes," mumbled Ashley. He didn't quite add "sir" to it.

"Lookin' for something?" enquired Dinny. "I might be able to help you. Got lots of stuff here," he added waving proudly around.

"I thought there might be something I could make a bench out of," blurted Ashley. "I was going to pay for it," he added anxiously.

"That all?" grinned Dinny. "You won't find much in there for a bench. Over here's the place. I'll show you. Come and have a look."

Ashley followed Dinny clumsily over the heaps to a staggering collection of boxes, boards, broken chairs and tables, sofas, stools, and other furniture.

"There's all sorts of stuff in there," said Dinny modestly. "It depends what you want the bench for, really."

"I think that table there would do," said Ashley, pointing to a small office-desk with two of the legs bent in.

"Okay, she's all yours. I'll get Watcher — that's me partner — and we'll shove it over the fence for you."

"How much is it?" asked Ashley reaching into his empty **pocket.**

"Forget it," said Dinny. "You can have it for a housewarmin' present."

"I don't mind paying, really."

"Garn, the thing's not worth much anyway. You might be able to do us a little favour some time, you never know."

"Anything you like," said Ashley without hesitation.

"I'm Dinny Virtue, by the way." And he held out his hand.

"Ashley Nash," said Ashley shaking it. "Pleased to meet you."

"Same here. Now we'll get this bench over the fence for you. I'll just see where Watcher is."

"I — I didn't want it today," said Ashley. "I have to find somewhere to put it."

"Okay. We'll bring it over tomorrow if you like."

"Thanks very much. I'm very grateful."

"See you tomorrow then."

"Yes. Thanks. Goodbye." And Ashley clambered quickly out of sight over the jumble of the yard towards his place.

That night Ashley Nash put his bed-wire and four boxes, his chairs, his table, and quite a number of other things back over the fence into Dinny's yard where he'd got them from.

Next morning Dinny and Watcher dragged out the desk Ashley had chosen and fixed up the legs for him. Then they carried it out the gate and round to Number 15. Leila helped them because of it being something of an event. A friendly neighbour in this neighbourhood was a rare thing.

Ashley met them at the door and they juggled the desk right into the house for him, in spite of his frantic assurances that he could manage it on his own, he wasn't ready for it yet, he didn't want it, and he was going to keep it for an outside bench. They put the table down in the kitchen and looked around the empty echoing house. A heap of blankets in one corner and dust in all the others was all that was there.

"You've got no furniture," said Dinny brilliantly.

"I'm having some sent," said Ashley unconvincingly. "It hasn't arrived yet."

"He's been living here all this time without a stick of furniture," said Leila accusingly to Dinny and Watcher, as though they should have known.

"We'll soon fix that," said Dinny. "We'll have this place fixed up with the best of everything before you can see which way it came from. Watcher, come with me."

Under the weakening protests of Ashley, Dinny and Watcher ranged across Dinny's yard, pulling out things as Leila called out what was wanted next and lowering them over the fence to Ashley and Leila. By sundown the house at Number 15 Essentry Crescent was fully furnished with a stunning variety of semi-serviceable furniture. A different lampshade in every room and two to spare. Pictures on the walls. Pots and pans under the sink. Mats on the floor. Blankets on all the beds. And an almost tearfully grateful neighbour.

From that time on their friendship with Ashley Nash grew along with the piles of perks they deposited in his yard for him to invent things with.

"I say, Tweek," said ex-Sergeant-Major Fulton. "Have you seen what they're doing across the road here? That blighter Virtue and his — er . . ."

"Of course I've seen," snapped Mr Tweek. "They've started putting their junk in the yard of Number 15."

"Might be quite harmless, of course," said the ex-Sergeant Major. "It may be just temporary."

"Temporary my foot!" snarled Mr Tweek. "Don't forget I saw how he started on his own yard. It's exactly the same. He puts a bit here and a bit there, and before you know it the whole place is one big mass of junk, getting higher and higher. It never stops."

"We can't have them turning the whole street into a junk yard," bombilated ex-Sergeant-Major Fulton. "Have to put a stop to it."

"How?" grated Mr Tweek.

"Well, there's always the authorities, Tweek. We'll simply have to explore all the avenues until we get satisfaction."

"And what avenues are there left to explore?" demanded Mr Tweek bad-temperedly. "I've even reported it to the owner of Number 15, and he won't do anything about it. If the owner won't complain nobody *can* do anything about it. But just let them break one regulation and I'll have them. And I've got a plan that's going to make them break the law without doing anything or being able to do anything about it."

"That's the spirit, Tweek. Fight fire with fire, by George. It's up to us to keep the street free from this kind of thing. What's this — er — plan of yours?"

"It can't fail," said Mr Tweek looking slyly around. "I might need your help, but we mustn't tell a single soul or it mightn't work. Now listen . . ."

In the Spring

NINE

IN THE SPRING

Leila was seeing a young man off at the gate. Watcher eyed him disdainfully.

"Third time that young Norman's been round here lately," he said. "First he wants a spindle-shaft for a hand-operated wood-drill, then it's a spacer-plate for a motorbike clutch, and now he's after a coupling for an over-sized ball joint. Must be mounting a wood-drill on a motorbike trailer or something."

"He's hangin' round after Leila, that's what he's doin'," said Dinny. "He asked me just now if he could take her out tonight."

"Bloody hell," said Watcher. "What did you tell 'im?"

"I didn't know what to tell 'im. Took me by surprise. Said he'd better ask Leila. I think she took 'im up on it. Don't know what's got into her. He looks like a cross between a cowboy and a Rosicrucian."

"That's the fashion these days."

"Hell!" was all Dinny could think of to say.

"He's got a flash car."

"Yeah. A car like that might just turn a girl's head. Wonder what made him pick on Leila? I didn't know she was all that attractive, did you?"

"Never took much notice, to tell you the truth."

"Well, we can't let it go too far. A bloke like that for a son-in-law wouldn't be much use to the organisation. In fact, he'd be useless."

"Can't stop her going out with him," said Watcher. "Not as if she was going to marry the bloke anyway. All girls her age go out with young blokes."

"Don't like the looks of it," said Dinny pessimistically. "I suppose she's got to go off sooner or later, but I was thinkin' of someone with a truck or something. That car of his would be useless in this game."

"He'll have a game of his own," said Watcher. "He's not the type to come into the organisation, even if he was invited."

"That means he'll probably whip Leila off before she has a chance to fill all her orders, and we'll get a bad name."

"No need to worry about it just yet," said Watcher. "We'll keep an eye on 'im and see if it calls for any action later."

"Do you think we ought to have a yarn with her about it?" asked Dinny.

"Like hell. That's the last thing we're going to do. We'll just follow them tonight and see how keen this young bloke is. If it looks serious we can try and head him off. But we mustn't let Leila get the idea we're buttin' in on her private affairs."

That night, when Norman's little Morris drove bravely out of Essentry Crescent under its load of banners, the scrapwaggon went charging after it. The oddly assorted convoy travelled along the main road into the city, but Dinny was too close. Norman saw the scrapwaggon following behind him, and asked Leila if her father and Watcher had intended going into town that night. Leila, who didn't know of the presence of the waggon right behind them, informed Norman that her father and Watcher never went out at night except on very special jobs. Then at some traffic lights the scrapwaggon got jostled right up behind Norman's little car, towering hungrily above it. The truck had had a blocked idling jet for the last day or two and Dinny had to keep revving the motor to keep it from stalling.

"Do you think they might have spotted us?" he asked uncomfortably.

"Everybody else in the street has," grinned Watcher.

"What'll we do?" asked Dinny with a trace of panic.

"Just pretend we're going the same way as them. We can explain something later."

So they followed the little car. Down the main street, round two blocks and back along the main street again. Norman was so flustered that he overshot the odd one or two parking places that were unoccupied. Then he couldn't stand it any longer and dashed off down a side-street and out around the unlit reserve at the edge of town. The baleful yellow headlights of the scrapwaggon roared after him.

"He's trying to give us the slip!" yelled Dinny, slamming the truck into second gear and juddering it around a corner after the terrified scuttling Morris.

"Don't blame him," said Watcher. "Better turn it in before we run the poor sod into the ditch. I think we've done our dash for this time."

They went back to Dinny's place for a conference and decided to say nothing about their night's work unless they absolutely had to.

"Have to leave things to settle down for a while after this little lot," said Watcher.

"We might have put 'im off already," said Dinny.

"It'd put *me* off," said Watcher.

"Wonder what Leila's going to say?" said Dinny uneasily.

"Have to wait and see."

So they opened a bottle of sherry and waited to see. Leila arrived home at a quarter past one in the morning, to find her two guardians still waiting to see what she was going to say. The sherry had obviously failed to fortify them. They greeted her with all the over-exaggerated surprise afforded someone who's been away for months and suddenly arrived back unexpectedly.

"Father," she began, "and you too, Watcher Amble; if you ever do that again . . ." She threw her green stole impatiently on to a chair-back.

"Do what again?" asked Watcher innocently.

"Yeah, *what?*" put in Dinny trying to look astonished.

"You know jolly well what I'm talking about," she cried. "Following us like that. I've never been so embarrassed. And poor Norman was so nervous we nearly had an accident. Our whole evening was ruined!"

"You've had plenty of time to recuperate," said Dinny pointedly, looking at his bare wrist.

"I've been having cups of tea with Norman's mother and father, if you must know. And I'm going there for dinner on Thursday night, so there."

She turned and flounced off to her room. Dinny and Watcher both reached for the wine bottle.

"Looks bad," said Watcher.

"We'll have to do something," said Dinny.

"We've done plenty already, if you ask me," said Watcher.

"Well I'm not having that young fancy-pants for a son-in-law," said Dinny, crashing his fist lightly on to the table. "And that's final."

"Okay," said Watcher resignedly. "I'll try and work out something tonight and let you know tomorrow."

Norman called for Leila on Thursday and trod up the path as though he might be ambushed at any moment from the tall junk that grew thickly on either side. He knocked on the door as though it could explode, and when Leila led him into the kitchen he might have been crossing a minefield.

"It's all right," Leila said. "You don't have to be nervous. Father and Mr Amble haven't said anything about you since I told them off about last Friday night. They're not here just now anyway, they went off somewhere half an hour ago."

"We've got him shook," said Watcher to Dinny behind their pile of old car-seats and bundles of baling-wire. "Now we'll shake him some more."

They tip-toed about their dirty work and slipped back into the tangle of the yard to watch the results of their handiwork from concealment. They got into position just in time before Leila and Norman came down the path.

Norman had an uneasy premonition that something was wrong as he reached to open the car door for Leila, but there was nothing he could have done about it by then anyway. As he opened the door there was a sudden angry *bzzz* inside the car and he slammed the door again quickly and jumped back. His car was full of blowflies. Hundreds of them. Thousands! Big bad-tempered bluebottles. Crawling all over the rugs and windows, steering-wheel, dashboard, windscreen and air-freshener. Thousands of blowflies.

Norman's courage was completely outnumbered. He ran this way and that for a few yards, shaking his hands as if the blowflies were all over him.

"Your car's full of blowflies," said Leila interestedly.

"It's never been full of blowflies before," Norman appealed to her. "What are they doing in there?"

"Trying to get out by the look of it," she said.

Norman rushed to the car, opened the door and waved his hand frantically into the roaring horde of agitated blowflies, with his averted face screwed up so tight it was going to be hard to get undone.

"That's not helping," said Leila impatiently. "You're shooing them all back in." She went round the car and opened all the doors. "Now for goodness sake, Norman, stand away. They'll go away on their own."

Norman stood blankly back and watched the droning exodus of

blowflies from his beautiful little car. The last few on the windscreen and rear window were going to have to be chased out individually.

"That's not fair," he said to her. "It's just not funny."

"I didn't put blowflies in your car," said Leila shortly. "It won't hurt the frilly thing anyway."

"It's not frilly," said Norman indignantly. "It's the best looked-after car in the whole district, I'll have you know. That's what."

"It's gaudy," said Leila.

"There's plenty of girls who'd be proud to be seen in that car," said Norman haughtily. "I notice you didn't mind riding in it the other night."

"It's ugly," said Leila.

"It happens to be the only car that colour in the whole city," said Norman. "It's distinctive."

"It's disgusting," said Leila.

"If that's the way you feel you won't be invited out in it any more," threatened Norman. "How do you like that?" he finished smugly.

"I do," said Leila. "I'm going home. You can get someone else to decorate your ugly little car."

And she went back to the house, leaving Norman hissing courageously at the last few stubborn blowflies in his car. He drove away with the job still uncompleted.

Dinny and Watcher strolled casually into the kitchen and got surprises to find Leila still there.

"Thought you were going out somewhere?" said Watcher.

"Hasn't your boyfriend come for you yet?" asked Dinny.

"Where did you get all those blowflies?" demanded Leila.

"What blowflies?"

"Yeah, what blowflies?"

"You both know very well what blowflies. Where did you get

them all from? That's what I want to know."

Dinny and Watcher glanced uneasily at each other.

"Put some ripe meat in a two-gallon jar," said Watcher.

"We let 'em breed up in there," said Dinny with a trace of pride.

"We put them in the young bloke's car for him to deliver for us," interrupted Watcher. "The lid must have come off." He trailed off weakly and they both waited for the blast from Leila.

"Well in future I don't want any help with my boyfriends. I can get rid of them myself, thank you."

"You mean you weren't serious about that young feller?" asked Dinny.

"Of course not," she said. "I wouldn't get serious about Norman. He's shorter than I am. He just pestered me until it was easier to go out with him and get it over with than keep on refusing. I'd have had him put off by now, if I'd been left alone to do it myself."

"Thought it might be something like that," lied Watcher, "but we didn't know if you'd be able to handle him on your own."

"Well in future just you remember that I *can*," said Leila firmly. "A woman has her own ways of handling situations like that, and cars full of blowflies isn't one of them."

"We — er — know it's none of our business," said Dinny, "but when we kick off all this'll be yours." He waved around at the tumbled heaps of junk that spread across the yard from corner to corner. "And we wouldn't like to see all we've built up over the years fall under bad management. We want you to marry a good businessman who's not frightened of a bit of hard work."

"Don't be silly, Father. I've got no intention of getting married off to anyone, and even if I had, there's only one man around here I'd dream of marrying, and there's little enough chance of that."

Just then Ashley Nash sidled up the path.

"G'day Ash. How's it going?"

"Fine, thanks. I think I've found a job you might like to have a shot at."

"Yeah? What's the guts of it?"

A friend of Ashley's had put culvert-pipes through the bed of a creek that ran through a block of land he'd bought on the edge of the city. He wanted several hundred yards of filling to level off the ground for a riding school he was starting up. He would pay ten bob a load for as much as they liked to bring. They went out to see the bloke and inspected the job. A verbal contract was taken out on the spot. It was the best job they'd got on to yet.

They were just getting the new filling job nicely organised when something they'd always half feared might happen, happened. Bilter caught them. Caught them red-handed.

They were travelling through the city with two hundred and fifty sheets of corrugated iron and a dismantled 500-gallon water-tank on the scrapwaggon, when they were pulled up by a traffic cop. He led them round to the Traffic Department weighbridge and found that they were almost as grossly overloaded as they looked. Then he informed them that he was also booking them for their load being a hazard to other traffic.

Dinny and Watcher had been prepared for a traffic offence ticket. The one who was driving, Dinny, produced his driver's licence, and Watcher gave his name as that of their boss, care of the City Council. But it didn't come off. The traffic officer rode with them round to the depot and dug up Bilter, who tried not to beam as he surveyed their load of iron.

"Thank you, officer. I'll deal with these chaps. If your department will just advise me what action is being taken." He wanted Dinny and Watcher to himself.

"In Gorman Street eh?" he almost chuckled. "With a load of

nothing but iron. On one of our trucks. I always knew you two were up to something, of course, and here's my proof. You're going to have a time trying to talk your way out of this one, aren't you?"

"No," said Watcher.

"Don't talk to me like that, Ambler, I warn you. This is going before The Committee. I'll tell you that before we go any further."

"Post our wages," said Watcher, turning to get his things out of the cab of the scrapwaggon. "We might as well get off to the pub, Dinny."

"Where do you think you're going?" demanded Bilter. "Come back here this instant! I haven't finished with you two yet by a long chalk!"

"Oh yes you have, Mr Bilter," said Watcher. "We're not staying here to be abused and bitched at by you for half an hour before you give us the sack. We're leaving right now."

"But you can't," insisted Bilter. "I haven't even sacked you yet."

"Well you're too slow. We've already left."

"Yeah, you missed out," put in Dinny, following Watcher towards the gate.

Bilter was still protesting as they passed out of earshot.

"D'you think he's going to kick up a stink?" asked Dinny.

"Don't know," replied Watcher. "He won't be able to resist telling his committee, but he hasn't got a single detail about it. That's why I made us walk out like that before he could ask any awkward questions. They'll probably just write us off their books and leave it at that. There's never been any complaints about our work, that's one thing in our favour."

"Well, what do we do now?"

"Wait. If nothing happens within a couple of weeks we'll know they're not going to do anything about it."

The Council posted the balance of their wages and holiday pay, and that was all. For the first week or ten days Dinny and Watcher were busy reorganising the organisation. Two hundred and eighty second-hand sheets of corrugated iron had to be found to fill the order Bilter had interrupted, so they hired a truck and collected the same lot from the Council tip and delivered it.

Then they went into the city, Dinny, Watcher, Leila and Ashley, to buy a truck of their own. For sentimental reasons they bought one the same year and model as the scrapwaggon they were so used to, and in a week or two it would have been hard to tell the difference.

Leila solved their immediate difficulties by pointing out: "You don't have to collect your filling a rubbish-tin at a time now. You can go straight to the Council tip and take your pick of all the best stuff."

"Can you do that?" asked Ashley doubtfully.

"Course you can," said Watcher. "People have been perking stuff from tips for hundreds of years."

"It's the born right of every citizen," added Dinny.

"I say, m'dear," said ex-Sergeant-Major Fulton, pondering into Felicity Cambert's front room, where she sat, as usual, at the window. "Tweek's sticking his neck out a bit far this time, isn't he?"

"Sticking his neck out?" asked Felicity politely.

"Yes, m'dear. Haven't you heard? I understand he's dug up some regulation saying you can't carry on a business within two hundred feet of a public park, reserve or playground. He's having his place officially declared free for public picnics and things. Says it'll force this Virtue blighter and Co. to pack up and clear out altogether."

"Oh," said Felicity.

"Yes, m'dear. Rather drastic, don't you think? Hope the fellow knows what he's doing. Wants it kept very hush-hush for the time being, but he's already begun negotiations with the authorities and got a very favourable reaction to this public park thing."

"A favourable reaction?"

"Yes, m'dear. I'd say it was the finish of this Virtue chappy around here. Can't say I've much sympathy for him really, after the shocking mess he's been making over at Number 15. Given a little more time they'd have had the whole street one great scrap-heap. It's got to stop somewhere."

"What a shame," said Felicity. "It'd be as dull as anything around here without Mr Virtue's yard. It's the most interesting thing in the whole street. I love to watch them with all their things. I think you and Mr Tweek should be ashamed of yourselves for trying to get them kicked out."

Ex-Sergeant-Major Fulton looked as though he'd suddenly become covered from head to foot with chilblains. As a matter of record he felt like it too.

"Er — yes. — Well well. — Quite — er. — Must be running along now. Mustn't fall behind, eh? — Ha ha! — Yes. — Well, 'bye now." And he blundered backwards out of the room. He always seemed to leave Felicity Cambert's house in confusion or embarrassment. Ex-Sergeant-Major Fulton made up his mind not to call on her quite so often in future.

If that woman was having some kind of joke with him, she'd better watch her step. Ex-Sergeant-Major Fulton wasn't to be fooled around with.

As he reached his gate the ex-Sergeant-Major met Harry Taggitt arriving home from work via the pub and the T.A.B.

"Any winners for Saturday, Fulton?"

"I say, have you heard about Tweek?" asked ex-Sergeant-Major Fulton on the spur of the occasion.

"What's he been up to now?" asked Harry uninterestedly.

"He's turning his place into a public playground," he said, with puzzled indignation. "What with that, and this Virtue blighter's rubbish-dump over the road the neighbourhood soon won't be worth living in. Should be something done to restrain them."

"Old Tweek's been running pretty wide on the turns lately," said Harry carelessly. "He wants swabbin' if y'arsk me." And he went on to his own place, next door to Mr Tweek's proposed public playground.

Watcher and Dinny had been on a tour of the excavation and construction jobs around the city and found several places where they could pull in among the officially-hired owner-driver trucks every now and again for a free load of filling. They tried it out with three sample loads and it worked perfectly. Then they picked up a hundred and fifty mended sacks and swung a deal with two 44-gallon drums of ex-navy insect repellent. A very satisfactory day all round. They went home early to tell Leila about it and found her sitting in the kitchen with Felicity Cambert, the pair of them talking away like auctioneers.

"What's up?" asked Dinny apprehensively.

"This is Miss Cambert, from just along the road," introduced Leila.

"We know," said Dinny. "More complaints about the yard?"

"Oh no," said Felicity. "I just popped over to tell you about Mr Tweek."

"What's he up to now?" asked Watcher.

"He's having his place made into a public park or something, so that nobody can carry on a business within two hundred feet of it. He told that awful Fulton person it would give him an excuse to have you closed down and shifted away."

"Tweek's always trying some caper like that. He's been at

it for years," said Watcher.

"This one sounds serious," said Dinny thoughtfully. He turned to Felicity. "How come you bothered tipping us off? I thought you were on Tweek's side."

"Tipping you off?" asked Felicity blankly.

"Why did you come and tell us about it?" asked Watcher.

"Don't be awful, you two," said Leila. "Miss Cambert has been very kind to warn us. There's no call for you to be rude."

"I was just telling Leila," said Felicity, "what fun it would be if we moved all your things over to my place. There's scads of space, and Mr Tweek wouldn't be able to do a thing about it. I'm not within two hundred feet of his public park."

"Thanks all the same," said Dinny, "but it's too big a job."

"It'd take months," said Watcher.

"Yeah. We'll have to work out some way of gettin' around Tweek without having to shift everything. But don't worry, we'll think of something."

"Well if you do need somewhere to put things you can always use my yard," said Felicity disappointedly.

"That's pretty decent of you, miss, but . . ."

"We have been thinking of starting a separate depot for the brass and copper and other non-ferrous stuff," said Watcher casually.

"Yes," said Leila. "Remember all that trouble we had sorting out the scrap for our new-truck money?"

"Yeah," said Dinny. "We're goin' to have to expand sooner or later. Sure you wouldn't mind, miss? We could pay you a little rent for the space. In the old days we used to back in and tip the whole load, if there was enough good stuff in it, but we've given that up now. We're gettin' selective. You'd only get the best stuff."

"I'd love it," said Felicity. "I've wanted heaps of things like yours ever since I came here."

Watcher and Dinny looked at each other with stretched, astonished faces, and suddenly they were all laughing.

Leila brought them back to earth. "But we still have Mr Tweek to deal with," she reminded them.

"Yeah," said Watcher. "We'd better ask Ash over for a conference tonight. He's the bloke next door," he explained to Felicity.

"Handles all our non-metal stuff," said Dinny.

"He's saving up to buy that house," said Leila. "The owner's going to let him have it cheap."

"Right then," said Dinny. "Conference here tonight after dinner. Perhaps Miss Cambert would like to come along? It might involve her yard."

"Felicity's staying for dinner," said Leila, "so she'll be here anyway."

Felicity giggled happily and within a few moments the two women were picking up conversational revolutions so fast that Dinny and Watcher retreated to Ashley's place for a preconference conference.

"If it comes to the worst we might have to get a lawyer," said Ashley when they'd told him about Tweek's latest threat to their organisation.

"Have to try and keep it from coming to that if we possibly can," said Watcher. "But I don't like the looks of it."

"There's bound to be something in the yard that'll help," said Dinny philosophically. "It's never let us down yet."

Ex-Sergeant-Major Fulton finished off a flask of brandy for morning tea, brushed his hair and his clothes, and called on Mr Tweek sucking a Lifesaver.

"I say, Tweek," he expostulated, "have you noticed anything odd about Miss Cambert recently?"

"No," snarled Mr Tweek ungraciously, "only that she's spent nearly every day this week over at Virtue's junk-yard. And that they've pulled her front fence down and driven their truck over the footpath into her garden with loads of their junk three times, and spread mud all over the public footpath and up the road. And put dirty old sheets of metal over the kerb — that's all I've noticed."

"You don't think she's actually — er — gone over to the other side, do you?" rumbled the ex-Sergeant-Major.

"Was she ever on our side?" demanded Tweek. "What did she do to help protect the neighbourhood from Virtue and his gang? Well, it doesn't worry me one little bit. They're all going to get what's coming to them when I spring my little surprise on them. After next Wednesday there's going to be a lot of changes made around here. And I'll have the law to back me up."

"Er — yes. Quite looking forward to it too," said ex-Sergeant-Major Fulton worriedly. "I must say it's been going on quite long enough. Can't understand Miss Cambert behaving like that, though. Just goes to show one can't be sure who one's friends are. It's just as well you didn't take her into your confidence, Tweek. She could have upset the whole scheme."

"How do you mean, upset the whole scheme?"

"Well — er — if she'd known about your intended — er — action, she might have forewarned this Virtue blighter. Thrown a spanner in the works."

"Well, she doesn't know about it, so she can't. You and I are the only ones who know anything about it. I've got them trapped at last and I'm going to be there to see Virtue's face when the police serve the order on him."

Leila and Felicity had been prospecting a new load of perks that Dinny and Watcher had tipped off the day before in Ashley's yard, and Felicity was crossing to her place with a big bulge of brass and copper in the front of her skirts, when she was intercepted by ex-Sergeant-Major Fulton.

"I say m'dear. You haven't mentioned anything to our friends over the road about Tweek's plan for next Wednesday, have you?"

"We're not interested in what Mr Tweek does," she said without stopping. "And I certainly haven't said anything to anybody about next Wednesday."

Injunction

TEN
INJUNCTION

On Wednesday morning ex-Officer Tweek triumphantly led an unwilling constable with a big envelope up Dinny Virtue's path. It was the first time Mr Tweek had ever set foot in the yard which had been haunting his waking and sleeping hours for nine years. He knocked on the door and stood back so that the first thing Dinny would see when he opened it would be the constable. It was.

"Hullo there, constable — Mr Tweek. Come on in. What can I do for you?"

The constable went into the kitchen and Mr Tweek had no option but to follow him. Watcher, Leila, Ashley Nash, and Felicity Cambert were all sitting around the table.

"Are you the proprietor of this — er — place?" the constable asked Dinny.

"Yeah, me and my partners here," said Dinny. "I'm the legal owner. What's up? You can talk in front of me friends."

"I have an injunction here," said the constable, unfolding his document, "restraining you from conducting a business within two hundred feet of a public park or reserve. I have to warn you that any further activities here will render you liable to arrest for contempt of a court order."

"And I'll be watching you, Virtue," crowed Mr Tweek. "You're finished round here, the whole lot of you. I've got another order being processed to make you clear all your junk out of sight of the street too."

It was obvious that the constable wasn't enjoying his job.

"I'll handle this, thank you, sir," he said to Mr Tweek. "I'm afraid he's right, sir. You will have to give up your activities in this neighbourhood. It comes under Section 14, Clause a of the Public Recreations Act, 1932. 'No person shall carry on, or cause to be carried on, a business within two hundred feet of a place set aside for public recreational purposes.'"

"Where's the public park around here?" asked Dinny.

"My place," said Mr Tweek. "I've donated the grounds to the Council for a public reserve."

"Good," said Dinny. "We must come over there for a picnic. But there must be some mistake," he continued, turning to the constable. "This isn't a place of business, it's an officially recognised charitable fund-raising organisation." Watcher passed him a letter which he handed on to the constable. "Here's the letter from the Government Department that sponsors the drive, accepting our offer to donate all our profits — after our wages and expenses, of course — to an officially recognised charity. And we're authorised to accept and pass on donations too, if you'd care to give a few shillings to the cause and help save some hungry child from malnutrition or something."

"I'm afraid that places a different complexion on the matter," said the constable to Mr Tweek, peering at the letter and then at his court order. "This law doesn't apply to non-profit-making organisations."

"Let me see that letter," snapped Mr Tweek, plucking it from the constable's hand. "It's dated the day before yesterday. You knew about this! You planned it. I'm going to take you to court for this. You're not getting away with it."

"That'll be enough, sir," said the constable firmly, taking the letter from Mr Tweek's trembling grasp and handing it back to Dinny. "I'll have to make a full report to my superiors about this, but I don't think you'll hear from us again, sir."

Mr Tweek made a very impolite and undignified exit. The

constable followed him more decorously.

"Well that's that," grinned Ashley.

"You're a genius, Ashley," smiled Leila happily. "It was all your idea."

And Ashley writhed in blushing embarrassment.

Not only did poor Mr Tweek's plan to have Dinny and Co. banished, bag and garbage, from Essentry Crescent go awry, but the method he used turned cruelly against him. The legalities had required him to publish notice in at least two news papers that his grounds had been declared open and free for public use, and to erect a sign. And it seemed that this was just the kind of informal locality that a number of Ladies' Guilds required for their multifarious social functions. It saved them cleaning up after themselves too.

In the first month no less than eleven meetings and tea-parties took place in the pleasant surroundings of Mr Tweek's front garden, and with such a perfect conversation-piece just across the road they were all a great success. This number was much less than the monthly average later became.

At first Mr Tweek attempted to attract sympathisers to his anti-Dinny and Co. cause, but he never got anywhere. And eventually he shut himself inside the house whenever a herd of cachinnating women trampled and littered his once flourishing gardens. He rudely refused all requests for extra chairs, hot water, or the use of his front veranda for a speakers' rostrum, but still they continued to use his place as what it had been proclaimed — public. There was a wedding reception that left the lawns and paths spottled for weeks afterwards with confetti. And a kindergarten mass-birthday-party that was practically the finish of Mr Tweek's lawn, flower garden and sanity.

During the holiday season there were several complaints about noisy parties carrying on into the early hours of the morning, and once the police were called to deal with something that resembled a brawl, which had broken out among Mr Tweek's shrubbery.

For some reason Mr Tweek could no longer bear the sight of ex-Sergeant-Major Fulton, and for some reason ex-Sergeant-Major Fulton could no longer bear the sight of Mr Tweek. Their relationship corroded to the point where they each pretended that the other never existed.

Perhaps the reason why Mr Tweek and ex-Sergeant-Major Fulton could no longer bear the sight of one another was because ex-Sergeant-Major Fulton had taken to blundering around the fringes of Dinny and Co.'s various departments until he'd blustered himself on to speaking terms with them by sheer brandied persistence. In fact they'd got to the stage where Dinny and Watcher had asked the ex-Sergeant-Major's advice about a load of ex-army motorbike and bren-carrier parts they'd bought up cheap. Ex-Sergeant-Major Fulton had somehow agreed to have the load temporarily deposited in his yard for him to go through and evaluate for them — for a small commission, of course.

Harry Taggitt had always kept his garden fairly tidy because tidy gardens were a bit of a fetish in Essentry Crescent. A kind of reaction against Dinny's yard, as nobody wanted to risk being accused of following his example. But when Ash Nash's yard fell under Dinny and Co.'s untidy influence, Harry began not to bother with his own grounds so much. Now that someone had set a precedent no one was likely to criticise him for neglecting his gardens and hedges a little. Then when Felicity Cambert followed Ash Nash's example so whole-heartedly, Harry Taggitt almost lost the interest he'd never had in gardening altogether. And when Mr Tweek, right next door to him, made his place into a public park and started having messy, noisy groups of people coming and going all the time, Harry didn't bother even mowing his lawns any more.

Then Harry struck a big win, paid off his back rent and nearly all his debts, and bought himself a Ford car of 1935 vintage. The third time he drove out in the car he returned in a taxi and the car followed next day at the back of a tow-truck. They put it on his front lawn for him to work on, and work on it he did. Whenever he wasn't racehorsing, Harry was either banging or tinkering with his car, or over at Dinny's yard, buying, borrowing or looking for something he needed.

Long grass grew up around the car and dismantled parts spread in an ever-widening radius. Harry had announced that he was going to "do the car up to the last nut and bolt", but if appearances were anything to go by the car was deteriorating faster than it was being done up.

The doing-up of Harry Taggitt's car had become more of a hobby than a project, but it assumed the proportions of a crime in Mr Tweek's averted estimation. He regarded Harry as a treacherous menace to everything decent and respectable, just like Dinny Virtue, and he never spoke a civil word to either of them again.

Leila and Felicity ramble contentedly on through their happily-littered lives, and in their spare time they're inexorably manoeuvring Ash Nash into romantic situations with Leila: ultimate, inevitable goal — marriage!

Ashley is using up all his spare time with his inventions, his goat, and paying off the deposit on his house. All his spare courage is needed for unsuccessful attempts to point out to Leila that there is no need to go to all that trouble.

Dinny and Watcher are the same perk-hungry, conference

holding pair they always were, except that they don't know what Leila and Felicity have in mind for Dinny as soon as Leila's safely married off to Ash Nash.

Dinny's neighbour on the right, as you face the road, who never speaks, still never speaks. He's built a two-foot-six extension on to the six-foot boundary fence, and wistfully pretends that Essentry Crescent is still the same as it was in the days before Dinny Virtue came to live there.